Corpsing

Kayleigh Marie Edwards

SINISTER
HORROR
COMPANY

PRESENTS

CORPSING

KAYLEIGH MARIE EDWARDS

Corpsing

First Published in 2017

Copyright © 2017 Kayleigh Marie Edwards

Cover artwork and design by Michael Bray.
MichaelBrayAuthor.com

ISBN: 978-1-9997418-3-9

SinsiterHorrorCompany.com

ACKNOWLEDGEMENTS

This collection, and several of the stories in it, would never have been created without Sinister Horror Company. The help, encouragement, feedback, and opportunity you guys have given me are invaluable, and so very much appreciated. I'd especially like to thank Justin Park for all your help – you are always just on the other end of a message for whatever I'm bothering you with!

Thank you to Michael Bray for his fantastic cover design and artwork, it really adds a lot to the book and encapsulates the 'feel' I was going for.

Jim Mcleod and David Saunderson – you have both helped me flex my writing muscles, and I've met so many people in the horror community through you both.

Nathan Robinson – the first writer I ever actually spoke to, read, and made friends with. Every time I lose confidence/fall into a procrastination trap, I remember how many more books you've written than me and it helps me get off my ass.

Mum. Thanks for proofreading and re-reading every story in this collection, and then buying everything I've ever had published! Also, thanks for reading all the rubbish that wasn't publishable in the end... god, how you've suffered.

Contents

BITEY

BACHMAN

Kayleigh Marie Edwards

Bitey Bachman

Brian rolled his eyes, swiveled his chair towards his desk, and stared at the security monitor. Everything was quiet so he refocused on his bag of sweets. He fished around for his favourite, the jelly ring, and slipped it halfway down his pinky.

Janet, his superior both in age and professional rank, put her hands on her hips and sighed. When Brian didn't respond, she stamped her foot. She had simply asked him to let the new girl shadow him from midnight when she was due to start her first shift, and in response, he had spent the last ten minutes ignoring her. Brian knew that the graveyard shift was the most practical time to train the new people as it was the quietest, and yet he felt the need to be awkward.

"Damn it, Bri!" she seethed.

3

"Damn it, Janet!" Brian exclaimed with a grin, spinning around to face her. He took the jelly ring off his finger and held it out. She groaned, throwing her hands in the air, and proceeded towards the door, knowing what was coming next.

"Damn it, Janet! I love you!" Brian sang, jumping out of his seat and following her out of his office.

"Just show Amy the ropes, and no practical jokes with this one, she's quite nervous," Janet said over her shoulder. Brian skipped down the corridor at her heels, waving the ring next to her face.

"Here's the ring to prove that I'm no joker!"

Janet quickened her pace, glancing left and right as she passed the resident's rooms. Some of their faces were pressed against the tiny, barred windows, watching the familiar scene. Brian performed his favourite musical every time he ate a bag of those damn sweets.

"Seriously Bri, I'm not in the mood tonight. My shoulder's killing me," she stopped walking and rotated her left shoulder, wincing to illustrate her pain. "Plus, we still haven't got through to Mr. Bachman's family yet, so the body's still here."

Brian looked to his right, where Bachman's door lay ajar. Through the gloom, he could just about see the outline of the sheet-covered body lying on the bed. He shuddered, and then refocused on Janet's shoulder.

"Sore?"

Janet nodded and then moved off again towards her office at the end of the corridor. Brian followed her, his brow crinkling, each line seeming to represent a thought.

"Why didn't you go home? You're injured."

"Because, Brian, we're short-staffed. It's just us, Frank, and Amy tonight. Plus, I've got a mountain of legal work to go over regarding Mr. Bitey Bastard Bachman's death," Janet fished in her white coat pockets for the keys to her office. "And on that note, not a word to Frank, the new girl, or anyone else about what happened. The last thing we need is a lawsuit."

They reached her office and she unlocked the door, fixing him with her serious look. He returned her gaze with a faux-serious expression of his own, unable to stop the corners of his mouth twitching upwards. She was an attractive woman but Brian thought that her 'serious look' wrinkled the corners of her mouth in a way that reminded him of prunes.

"Wipe that look off your face, Bri. Seriously, you did… get rid of that syringe, didn't you?" Janet whispered, her eyes darting down the corridor as though someone were lurking in the shadows, ready to record the secret.

"Yup," Brain nodded. Janet mimicked the movement.

"Good, and the case of…?"

"I dumped it in a bin out back and set fire to the lot," Brian assured her, winking. "What was that stuff anyway? How did it get mixed up with the infirmary delivery?"

"It was supposed to go to the research lab downstairs," Janet muttered, distracted by her shoulder pain. Brian looked around.

"Downstairs? We're on the ground floor?"

Janet's eyes widened as she realised her big-mouthed blunder. Brian laughed.

"Oh come on, you're not seriously telling me there's a secret basement with a research lab?"

"If that gets out, it'll be your job, Bri. The lab's just an extension of the hospital next door, it's nothing to do with us, and I don't know what they do down there. Just the usual, I expect. Even so, it's on a need-to-know basis, understand?" Janet said, her tone slicing his amusement right out of the air.

"A secret basement research lab? In an insane asylum?"

5

Janet nodded, looking around again. Brian chuckled. She looked at him and sighed.

"What's so funny?"

"It's ridiculous. Like something out of one of those crap horror films. What next? Vampires in the attic? Bodies buried in the walls?" Brian smiled.

"This is serious…"

"Don't worry, boss. I won't say a word, not that anyone will ask. No one's going to investigate the death of a murderer," Brian rested a hand on her shoulder, intending to extend some comfort. Janet jumped back with a shriek and batted his hand away.

"Sorry, I forgot about the stitches."

"Idiot," she muttered, stepping into her office and closing the door in his face. Brian smiled at her silhouette through the frosted glass, and turned back down the corridor, whistling The Time Warp.

He'd been working for Janet for a good twenty-something years, and enjoyed their love-hate relationship. True, the hate mostly came from her end, but he knew she was fond of him deep down. She just didn't know it.

The whistle turned into singing and dancing as Brian meandered past the rows of faces peering out at him.

"It's just a jump to the left…"

On the outside, he was enjoying his well-practiced musical moment, but on the inside, he couldn't get his bizarre morning out of his head.

He had turned up for his morning shift at six and began his rounds. Most of the residents were fast asleep then, so he yelled at them through their little windows. He supposed it was mean, but their faces as they were startled into consciousness were so amusing. Janet insisted that because of their mental disorders, they weren't entirely responsible for the actions that had landed them in Flagg's Ranch (the name of the asylum had always bothered him: it was previously an American-style riding stable before a mental institution, yet the site hadn't been renamed). Brian had no prejudice against them for their mental disorders; it was their heinous and violent crimes that he could never really get his head around.

In the grand scheme of despicable crimes against humanity, you name it and at least one of them had done it. Brian wasn't among the staff that thought they deserved nice, cosy lives, though he wasn't cruel. Irritating was what he was going for – merely an annoyance. He liked to wake them up, and jump out from around corners to startle them. Sometimes he'd take bites out of their desserts and then tell them they'd done it themselves, just for the heck of the confusion it caused. He thought they deserved some form of punishment on society's behalf, but there was no real malice behind his 'attacks'.

"And then a step to the ri-i-i-i-ight!" Brian sang, sliding down the hallway. "You put your hands on your hips…"

During his rounds, he had come across Bachman, who claimed to feel sick. Brian didn't believe him and tried to get him back into bed. After all, Bachman was always lying about ailments to get into the infirmary. Brian thought he had a sweet spot for Mary, the on-site nurse.

Brian wrestled with Bachman and managed to get him under the covers, but before he could leave the room the old man was up again, clutching his stomach and dry retching. Brian shut the door on him, then Bachman started screaming bloody murder through his window, disturbing the other residents. Brian knew from experience that once one of them started screaming, others would follow suit, and the next thing you knew you'd be making the rounds armed with sedatives. Janet knew it too, because she bolted from her office the second Bachman's first syllable ricocheted off the walls and into her ears.

"I'm going to be sick!" Bachman cried, as Janet pushed past Brian, flung open the door, and entered the room. He backed away as soon as she and Brian took the first step towards him.

"It's okay Mr. Bachman, you'll feel better after a nice lie down," Janet nodded towards the bed. Bachman stared at her with narrowing eyes and shook his head.

"But I don't want to go to bed."

Brian gritted his teeth, feeling Janet soften next to him. For someone who'd worked in mental health her whole life, she could be so easily manipulated. Well, he couldn't.

"I'm not having your crap today Bachman, get into bed."

"I need Mary," Bachman insisted, stepping back against the wall.

"Mr. Bachman…" Janet started, taking another step.

"I need Mary!"

"Just calm…." Janet pleaded, aware of the dozen or so pairs of feet shuffling towards the windows in the other rooms.

"Mary! I want Mary!"

"Mary, Mary, quite contrary!" Fred Rice squealed, from inside his room. Brian squeezed the bridge of his nose and closed his eyes.

Rice, in particular, bothered him. To an amateur, the guy seemed completely insane, but Brian knew the difference between genuine insanity, and an insanity plea bargain. In Brian's opinion, there was nothing wrong with Rice apart from his morals – the crimes that had landed him at Flagg's Ranch were unspeakable. He also loved to aggravate the others.

"Put a sock in it, Rice!" Brain boomed. Rice stared across the corridor and through Bachman's door at him with his face squashed against the bars, grinning from ear to ear. He chuckled.

"Bachman freaking out again?" Rice smirked. Brian recognised his expression. Thanks to Bachman's monthly outbursts, everyone on the floor was privy to his deepest fear – the fear that had led him to the asylum in the first place. He had killed his next-door neighbour on the night of a full moon.

"Rice, I'm warning you. Don't... you... dare."

Rice backed away from the door and Brian relaxed. The second he did so, a wolf-like howl pierced the ward. On hearing the howl, Bachman screamed, then another scream from somewhere else on the ward followed. Janet took in a deep breath.

"Oh crap! Bri, get to the infirmary and ask Mary for Mr. Bachman's usual dose of Diazepam!"

Brian nodded and took off, shooting a furious glance at Rice's room as he went. Rice was too busy imitating the creature of the night that Bachman so feared to notice, but Brian vowed to deal with him later.

"Mary!" Brian burst into the infirmary. He scanned the room, noting the closed bathroom door. He strode across the room and banged on it. "Mary?"

After a short delay, a small voice responded from within.

"Uh, yeah?"

"We've got a situation."

There was another pause.

"Mary?"

"I'm on the toilet, sir," Mary's voice was clipped by simultaneous embarrassment and annoyance.

"Well can you hurry up? Bachman's losing his shit again and he's setting off the whole floor."

"I can't... go... with you listening on the other side of the door!" Mary explained, discomfort loading every word.

"I'll just wait by the medicine cabinet then."

Brian walked to the opposite side of the room and leaned back against the counter, tapping his foot. A moment later, Mary coughed.

"Sir, you're killing me here! I need a few minutes!"

"But we need you to shoot up old Bachman and then knock the rest of 'em out!" Brian protested.

"The Diazepam's in a box on the counter, just grab a dose. Syringes are in the top cupboard," Mary instructed, her discomfort growing more evident with each passing second. Brian turned to the counter. Two new delivery boxes sat atop, both opened.

"But I'm not qualified to…"

"Brian, for God's sake, this isn't a wee! Get the hell out!" Mary cried, the heat of her blazing embarrassment suddenly filling the room. "I'll be there in a few minutes!"

Brian crinkled his nose in disgust of the information he now regretted receiving, and quickly checked the labels on the boxes. He squinted, realising he'd left his glasses in his car, but they both seemed to spell the same thing. He grabbed a vial and a syringe and fled from the infirmary before he heard something else he didn't want to.

By the time he got back to the ward, all hell had broken loose. A chorus of howls was reaching fever pitch in a battle against an opposing symphony of terrified screams. Rice was peering out of his window, silent and appearing to enjoy the madness he'd created. Brian ran into Bachman's room, fiddling with the syringe wrapper as he went.

Janet was trying to force Bachman down onto his bed. Brian handed the sedative and syringe to her and took over. He managed, though with difficulty, to overpower the little old guy and get him lying down.

"Where's Mary?" Janet asked, loading the syringe.

"I've got him pinned, jab him!" Brian commanded,

10

struggling despite Bachman's frail frame and age; he could be a handful when he was all riled up.

"What? I can't do it, it's supposed to be the nurse," Janet protested, holding the syringe like it was suddenly the enemy.

"She's on the crapper, Jan'!" Brian barked. "And don't give me that regulations bollocks, I've seen you do it plenty of times!"

The howls and screams from the ward were becoming deafening, and Bachman was actually starting to wriggle free. Brian stared at Janet, motioning with his head for her to jab Bachman. She shook her head.

"I've only done it in emergencies!"

"This is a blasted emergency!" Brian cried, barely audible above the hysteria. Janet hesitated and then clambered onto the bed and rested her knees on Bachman's forearm. She slapped his inner elbow with the back of her fingers, located a vein, and maneuvered the needle into it, plunging the sedative into his blood stream.

It took a minute or two for the drug to take effect, but finally Bachman let his eyes close and the tension left his body. Mary appeared in the doorway a moment later with a trolley loaded with sedatives.

"Sorry for the delay!" she yelled. "Where do you want me to start?"

"Start with Rice," Brian replied, trying and failing to hide his smirk from Janet. "In fact, I'll help you."

He rose, patted Janet on the back, and left the room. He unclipped his keycard from his belt as he crossed the corridor with Mary.

"Feeling relieved?"

Mary looked at him, without understanding his meaning at first, then flushed red.

"Oh shut up!"

A completely unfamiliar scream interrupted them. They

11

turned as Janet stumbled out of Bachman's room, clutching her shoulder. Blood seeped out between her fingers, staining her blouse. Panicked, she ran into Brian's arms. Bachman appeared a moment later, looking up and down the hall.

"Jesus Christ," Brian muttered, taking in the sight of him. Blood covered the lower half of his face and dripped off his chin. He looked entirely confused. Brian wasn't surprised; the old man wasn't normally a biter, let alone a cannibal.

"You crazy bastard! What are you doing?"

"I…I don't know…what's going on?" Bachman gasped, his eyes rolling a little. He wobbled forwards.

"Stay back, Bachman!" Brian warned, fingering the taser in his pocket. It was completely against the rules, but Brian had used it to save Janet from a crazed and extremely violent resident a decade ago, and so she looked the other way. That was the only time Brian had used it and he only kept it on his person in case of a life or death scenario, but he didn't like the look in Bachman's eye.

Bachman ignored the warning, stumbling towards them. Brian gripped the taser, about to yank it from his pocket, when Bachman's eyes suddenly rolled all the way back and he crumpled to the floor, unconscious. Brian brushed Janet's hair over her shoulder, inspecting the wound, and gently nudged her towards Mary.

"Fix her up and radio me if she needs to go the hospital," Brian instructed. "I'll deal with him."

Mary led Janet away, and Brian approached Bachman's unmoving body. On closer inspection, Brian noticed that the old man wasn't unconscious at all – he was dead. His old features were still contorted by confusion rather than relaxed by the peace that death usually allowed. For the first time, Brian felt a stab of sympathy for a resident.

An hour later, Janet had sent Mary home (apparently there was something wrong with her stomach), and she and

Brian were sat in the infirmary puzzling over Bachman's death. After much debate, Janet's eyes fell on the two open boxes on the counter. She walked towards them, reading the labels. One was Diazepam, and the other was something else beginning with a 'D' that she had neither seen before, nor could even pronounce.

"Brian, what was in the syringe we stuck in Bachman?"

"Diazepam, like you said," Brian replied, though he already had that bad feeling creeping in. Mistakes in places like this tended to end up on the news.

"Did you take it from this box?" Janet asked, pointing to the one on the right. Brian nodded, relieved, assuming she was pointing to the correct box. Janet's face pruned.

"You idiot! Did you even read the labels?"

Janet fiddled with the open lid flaps of the offending box, muttering to herself. Something on the lid caught her eye, and she pressed all the flaps closed, groaning.

"Oh no! Oh... oh... shit!"

Brian then knew it was serious – Janet reserved swearing only for the direst of circumstances. Brian joined her at the counter, sucking in a breath as he saw the black and yellow tape and the biohazard sticker.

Now, at nine at night, Brian was skipping down the corridor, driven a little loopy himself by the morning's bizarre incident and his own tiredness. The warden who was scheduled to relieve him had called in sick, and Mary's embarrassing stomach upset prevented her from returning for the second half of her split shift. The other staff were in the women's wing because one of the residents there was due to give birth, and newbie Amy wouldn't arrive for a few more hours. Unwilling to leave an injured Janet in the lurch, Brian offered to stay on. By the time he got out of there he would have worked a full twenty-four hours, but he figured there was no point in whining about it.

"You put your hands on your hips!" Brian wiggled his hips as he brought his hands to them. "And bend your knees in ti-i-ight!"

He lowered his voice as he approached Rice's room, having no desire to interact with the little sod.

"And it's the pelvic thru-u-u-ust, that really drives…"

"Drives you insa-a-a-a-ane!" Rice screeched. Brian let his hands fall from his hips, shooting Rice a look that threatened to turn into a punch.

"Very funny," Brian grumbled.

"Let's do The Time Warp aga…."

"Shut up Rice, you've ruined it."

Brian stormed into his office, no longer in the mood for The Time Warp or anything else for that matter. He hated Rice, now even more for ruining his singsong and his enjoyment of Rocky Horror. It was inevitable he would grow to hate it anyway; he eventually grew to hate everything introduced to him by his ex-wife. As far as she knew, he never liked it anyway. He wasn't going to admit to her that he actually enjoyed a musical about cross-dressers - he was a rugby fan, for crying out loud. He didn't care what the people at the asylum thought though, he could always point out they were insane if they blabbed.

At about quarter to midnight, Brian awoke from an accidental nap in his office. His eyes flew to his monitors, half-expecting to see some disaster unfolding, but all was well. Just to make sure he hadn't missed anything, he radioed Frank in the security hut. There was nothing to note, and Amy hadn't turned up yet, which Brian was glad about. With any luck she wouldn't turn up at all and then he wouldn't have to drag her inexperienced ass around all night. The only thing worse than being short-staffed was being short-staffed and trying to train someone clueless.

Brian drummed his fingers on his desk, considering doing something he shouldn't. He decided that he didn't care about the rules and would take a little personal time to shower, since it was approaching his eighteenth hour on the job. It would either wake him up a bit or relax him into a second nap but either way, there really wasn't much going on anyway.

He unbuckled his belt and left it, along with his radio and taser, on his desk, and slipped out of his office. He kept his eyes on Janet's office as he crept towards the shower room, which was right next door to it. Janet's light was off, which meant, Brian hoped, that she was taking a little personal nap time of her own.

He reached her office and peered through the frosted glass. He could just about make out the shape of her sat in her chair, slumped over her desk. Brian smiled; she was snoozing. He tiptoed into the shower room.

"Touch-a, touch-a, touch-a, touch me! I wanna be dir-ir-ty!" Brian sang, soaping his armpits. He had no idea how long he'd been in the shower, but he had managed to make it through half the soundtrack. "Thrill me, chill me, fulfill me! Creature o-of the night!"

As if on cue, the fire alarm sounded. Brian jumped, dropping the soap. He watched it slide towards the drain, smirking at a prison joke he'd heard once, before remembering what had made him drop it in the first place.

He stepped out of the shower stall, reaching for his towel and wrapped it around his waist. He wiped the steam off the mirror and sighed at his own reflection; it was probably a false alarm but he was going to have to check, and in the process he would more than likely get an earful from Janet.

The mirror was already steaming back up when he heard the footsteps squelching up behind him. He turned, wondering how Janet would have thought to look for him in the men's shower room, preparing to crack a joke about her hoping to catch him with his junk on display.

The playful grin dropped from his face when he saw her; it was Janet... but it wasn't. Blood and puss seeped through her shirt at her shoulder, congealing around her throat. She stared at him with glazed white eyes. She barely had pupils, but they were fixed on him anyway. She reached out as she sloped towards him, a low gurgle escaping her throat.

"So, it's finally happened. You owe me twenty bucks," Brian sighed, genuine sadness mixing with his wager victory. "If I'm not mistaken Janet, you are a zombie now, are you not?"

Janet groaned, almost closing the gap between them. Brian shook his head, beginning to side step her but making no sudden movements.

"And to think, you said having a zombie apocalypse plan was ridiculous."

Brian stared at her, fighting the tears. He had been friends with Janet for so many years; she had even been the subject of jealousy-fuelled arguments between him and the ex. A thought flashed to Brian's mind and a giggle escaped him – of all the inappropriate moments for it to happen, a scene from Brian's favourite show had entered his brain. He reached out and rested a hand on her good shoulder.

"I'm sorry this happened to you," he quoted, with genuine sincerity. She snapped her teeth, almost catching his fingers before he managed to yank his hand away. "For God's sake, keep a grip on yourself Janet!"

She lurched forward again, reaching with both hands towards his crotch. Brian jumped almost out of reach.

"Whoa, easy!"

Janet grabbed and gnawed at the towel for a second, before realising it wasn't flesh. Brian considered the risk of trying to retrieve it and was about to make an attempt, when

Janet snapped her teeth together again. With an embarrassing whimper, Brian retreated from the shower room, closing the door behind him as he backed into the corridor.

"Freeze!"

Shivering, Brian turned towards the shaking voice.

"Not much choice."

He cupped his hands around his modesty, examining the unfamiliar face. He nodded as it occurred to him that she must be Amy. She was young, probably just out of university, with wide, scared eyes. The alarms raged on, but barely drowned out the now raging residents.

"What's going on here?" Brian asked, attempting to assert some authority.

"How did you get out of your room?" Amy asked, her eyes darting to the locked doors lining the corridor. She noticed Bachman's open door. Brian caught the assumption in her eyes as she pieced together what she thought was happening.

"What? I'm not a resident!"

Brian shifted his weight as his nerves prickled. He could hear Janet fumbling with the door handle behind him. He took a few steps forward. Without warning, Amy tugged a taser out of her pocket. Brian stopped in his tracks, holding up both hands. Her eyes fell to his crotch, but only for a second and quite involuntarily. Her cheeks turned crimson.

"What do you think you're doing, taking my personal things from my office?" Brian barked, annoyed by the cheek of it.

"I don't want any trouble," Amy all but whispered, ignoring him. "Just go back to your room and everything will be fine."

"Listen, I don't have time for this. It's going to come out of the bathroom any second and I don't want her gobbling my danglies off!" Brian exclaimed, suddenly very nervous as he heard the latch click behind him. "Although I can't lie, it's not like the thought never crossed my..."

"What's going to come out of the bathroom?" Amy interrupted, inching in his direction as though he wouldn't notice.

"The zombie of course!" Brian exclaimed. The shower room door creaked. "Give me my taser, quick!"

Amy just gave him a look that conveyed sympathy for his mental state. Brian sighed, finally getting an idea of how patronised the residents must have felt each time he shot that look at them himself.

"It's okay, I work here!" he insisted. He could hear the door opening, slowly but surely. Amy nodded, smiling.

"Of course you do, sweetie."

Brian groaned; he was just going to have to go around her. Unwilling to wait to be eaten alive, Brian made a dash past her, his legs moving faster than he imagined they could. He was quite literally running balls out down the corridor. Unfortunately, Amy must have been some cross-track champion or something because she was on him in an instant.

Brian hit the ground before he even realised the jolt to his spine was his own goddamn taser. He spasmed, cursing himself for underestimating the stupid newbie.

"Stop tasing me!" he managed to yelp, as she upped the voltage and stabbed him again. "Argh!"

Brian saw stars, then what looked like that white noise on the television, and then everything went black.

He woke up in a familiar, yet disturbing place - Bachman's room. Only, Bachman wasn't in it. Brian doubted the body had been moved during his shower break, and he had a feeling the old dude was up and about enjoying a new lease of life. And probably someone's innards by now, too.

Wincing as he rose, he stretched his seized up muscles and went to the door, pressing his face to the tiny, barred window. He grimaced, locking eyes with Rice, who grinned back from the room directly opposite him.

"Welcome to the nut house!" Rice yelled, over the still ringing alarm and hysterical residents. Amy cut their eye contact as she ran past.

"Hey!" Brian yelled. "Where's Janet?"

Amy returned, panting.

"She..." Amy lost her wording and pointed in the direction of the exit.

"If there's a fire, you have to let us out," Brian reasoned. Amy shook her head.

"No fire. The alarm was set off from the security hut. I just went out there..." Amy trailed off, her pupils dilating as she remembered some horrible image.

"Frank?" Brian asked, though he had a feeling he knew why his old pal had set off the alarm. Poor bastard probably had Bachman's teeth in him before he knew what was coming, and the alarm panel was right there on the security desk.

"I found him slumped over his desk, he... he bit me!" Amy pointed at her shin. Brian nodded, piecing the whole scene together. At some point, Bachman had got up and made his way outside, finding Frank. He had proceeded to eat the only security guard on duty, who must have conveniently slumped over onto the fire alarm button. Meanwhile, Janet was doing a little rising from the dead of her own, probably killed by Bachman's infected bite and reanimated by the alarm.

Brian smiled at Amy in the sympathetic way she had only ten minutes before smiled at him. Poor thing probably had no idea that she would be the next one to bite the dust... then bite someone else. It suddenly occurred to Brian that the incident was no longer contained; Bachman was out on the prowl, and by now Frank and Janet probably were too.

Brian closed his eyes, gathering his mental resources – he knew what he had to do. It was finally time, after all his years of bored daydreaming, to put his zombie apocalypse plan into action. Amy snapped him out his thoughts.

"Oh my God!"

She pulled her blood-covered hand away from her leg.

"It's my first shift and everyone's dead! How am I meant to shadow them if they're dead?"

"Go, ergh, argh!" Brian suggested, stretching his arms out rigidly and adopting a corpse-like expression. Amy neither laughed, nor even acknowledged his hilarious joke. Her face crumpled.

"What do I do?"

"Listen, Amy is it?" Brian said, in his most authoritative, yet soothing, tone. "I'm Brian and I really do work here. There's no time to explain why I'm naked, but I need your help. Go into my office, and get my keycard from my desk drawer. You'll see my picture attached to it. Bring it back to me."

Amy nodded and darted off, returning mere seconds later.

"You really are staff," she mumbled, studying his picture. "I'm so sorry I…"

"Don't worry about it," Brian interrupted, pushing his fingers through the bars of his window. Amy went to swipe the card on the wall panel.

"Whoa! What are you doing?"

Amy froze just before swiping the card.

"I thought you wanted me to let you out?"

Brian shook his head and wiggled his fingers. Amy slowly handed the card to him and he snatched it away.

"Are you mental? I'm not going out there! We're in the

zombie apocalypse, in case you haven't noticed? I'll let myself out when the coast is clear but until then I'm lying low."

Amy nodded, her eyes darting up and down the corridor. She noticed something that made her eyes widen even more, and turned back to Brian with a pleading expression.

"Quick, let me in!"

"No can do. You're already bitten, I'm afraid."

"But…"

"You're being very selfish," Brian sighed. "Don't drag me down with you! Now get out of here before you lure them all this way!"

Amy hesitated for a moment, then darted towards the exit. Brian turned and leaned against the door, shrugging his tense shoulders. There wasn't much he could do for the moment, so he decided to have another nap.

The next day, when the police arrived for his statement, Brian had to admit, if only to himself, that he was a little disappointed. He was told that an emergency call had come in from new staff member Amy, explaining that crazed cannibals were on the loose. When the authorities arrived, they found an old man, a security guard, a woman in a white coat, and a young lady in uniform heading towards the brightly lit hospital next door. Instead of cooperating, they decided to attempt to have a police picnic. The officers, having been familiarized with zombies, thanks to popular culture, had recognised them for what they were and immediately bashed their brains in. Brian hadn't foreseen that; in the movies, no one ever seemed to recognise the zombies. They normally just stood there wondering what they were until they were gnawed and infected.

As he made his way to the morgue to identify the bodies, Brian cursed the movies for lying to him; no matter how slow moving they were, the zombies always managed to amass in hordes and take over. In boring reality, they were just too slow to achieve world domination, and had been swiftly dealt with. Brian hadn't even got to enjoy phase two of his plan; acquire a boat.

He cheered up a little later, remembering that there was a secret research lab in the basement. He broke into a grin as he realised that he was now probably the only one left in the building privy to that information.

He thought of his ex-wife, a woman whom he'd often fantasised about stabbing with a needle of Diazepam. Or horse tranquilizers. Perhaps, if he found his way into that lab, he'd find another batch of something far more amusing than a sedative to use on her. Brian thought of his dream boat, sighing. Perhaps there was hope for his apocalypse/retirement plan after all.

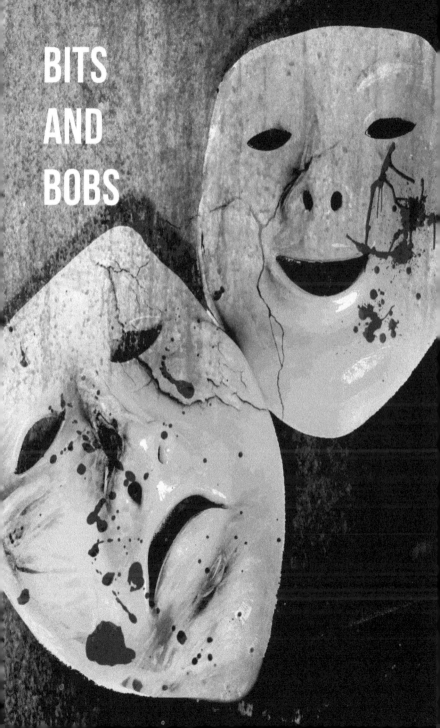

BITS

AND

BOBS

Bits And Bobs

Steven Plunkett stared at Doctor Leanne Linstrum's expression from his side of the desk, and groaned inside. He had seen that same expression on a dozen faces over the last couple of years, and he knew what was coming. All remaining hope of his dream plummeted to the pit of his stomach. *Don't say it*, he thought, staring at her forehead as he willed her to change her mind. *Just don't say it.*

"I'm sorry Mr. Plunkett, we just feel that this isn't a good fit for you." Doctor Linstrum cocked her head to the side in that oh-so-sympathetic way he had seen so many times. He closed his eyes, feeling the tears rise up his throat. Steven rubbed his palms on his knees, leaving damp imprints, and smiled a tight-lipped smile. *Just leave,* he commanded himself. *Keep your dignity.*

He rose to his feet, steadying himself as his heart pounded in his ears. It was knocking so hard against his ribcage that he wobbled a little as he stood. He turned and shuffled towards the door, his shoulders hunched as they always were, and turned back towards her. She smiled with sympathetic eyes and opened her mouth, about to say something.

"Well fuck you then," he said, and then sloped out of her office, taking care to avoid eye contact as her mouth dropped open. *Damn it! I said, keep your dignity!* Steven scolded himself.

Steven hadn't been in Tennessee for long, and already his trip was wasted. As a child, he had been obsessed with all things morbid. As a teenager, he'd had his first taste of the life he wanted when he completed a fortnight's work experience at a funeral parlour. As he entered his adult years, he grew to accept that he didn't have the mental capacity to professionally delve into the field of the dead. Instead, he took a job as a porter at a local hospital, which he loved. Sometimes he got to wheel bodies in and out of the morgue. But the Body Farm, now that really was the cream of the crop.

The Body Farm was a unique place in the U.S where unclaimed bodies were laid out in the grounds and left to be studied as they decomposed. Crime scenes were constructed to train CSI teams, and at any given time there would be around forty bodies. Steven, whose desire to become a part of the scene, had flown from the UK and volunteered as a porter there. Though Dr. Linstrum had found his request to volunteer odd, free labour was free labour and she wasn't about to turn it down. Unfortunately for Steven, just like with every place he'd donated his time, they had found a reason to dismiss him. Perhaps they didn't like his humour.

Standing outside the gates to the farm, shrouded in the cover of night, Steven decided that he'd had enough. This was his dream, and if those bastards insisted on giving him the boot, he'd donate a little something other than his time. Something for them to remember him by.

He was aware that there was a huge crime-scene reconstruction already staged for the following morning, all ready and waiting for a brand new batch of trainees. It was meticulously coordinated and organised; severed body parts had been strewn and 'murder' weapons had been concealed. The trainees were facing a timed crime puzzle. Well, Steven smiled, he'd just add a little unexpected detail to the mix - give the apparent 'experts' something to really mull over.

After scaling the wall, Steven dropped into the farm and staggered around the tree line taking care to avoid the security cameras. He burped, tasting the concoction of alcohol he'd spent the last few hours drowning his sorrows in, and proceeded to familiarise himself with the scene before him. It was a double-homicide; both were female victims with some of their organs removed. The organs, Steven guessed, were scattered around the ground ready for the training team to locate.

"Sshhtupid Linstrum," Steven muttered, unzipping his jeans and pushing them down to his ankles. He stood there for a moment, swaying proudly with his nether regions exposed, smirking. He took his trusty penknife from his pocket, stumbling a little as he tried to coordinate his hand. With the alcohol and the cold, he was beginning to feel rather numb.

He chuckled to himself as he got to work. His plan was genius – no – inspired, he thought. When the team got there in the morning, they'd go about their simulated investigation. At some point they'd start to solve the murder mystery, and then one of them would stumble upon his donation to the cause. If they weren't going to let him be part of their precious system, then he was going to bring it down, if only for the day. Steven laughed at his own amazing idea as he tossed his testes into the trees.

"Figure that one out," he slurred, his smugness enveloping him like a warm blanket. Mere seconds later, Steven realised that it wasn't the warmth of smugness that was spreading through his limbs, it was the searing pain emanating from his groin. He looked down at his self-mutilated manhood, and let out a whimper. All of a sudden, he wasn't feeling so drunk and all of a sudden, this didn't seem as funny.

He meandered like a cowboy into a clearing where he knew security would see him on their monitors, hoping that at the very least, an ambulance would get to him before he bled out. And then he heard the barking. Steven froze, pressing both hands to his modesty, as though the fast-approaching canines would judge him otherwise. How, in all his research about this place, could he have forgotten that this was also where they train cadaver dogs? Cadaver dogs that are also used for security, and released once the silent alarm is tripped because - and he had learned this in the first week - only a lunatic would break into the Body Farm at night.

Steven Plunkett was discovered shortly after his demise; he hadn't stood a chance against the dogs. In a small way, however, he had gained a victory. Thanks to the clean up of his own body interrupting the training exercise, his testes hadn't been discovered for four days, really throwing a spanner in the works for the trainee team. Everything ground to a halt as the experts struggled to separate bits of Steven from the planted body parts.

Somewhere, Steven groaned – so much for keeping his dignity.

SIREN

Kayleigh Marie Edwards

Siren

Lucy Black didn't like her new house, and she had told her mother as much. Her complaints fell on deaf ears; her mother, Julia, was going through a divorce and insisted that they were lucky to find a nice, lakeside house, especially at such short notice.

Of course, had Julia seen the little girl that lived in the lake, she might have reconsidered.

* * *

Lucy always hated moving house, but this was the worst move by far. In her eleven years of life, Lucy still hadn't quite grasped the concept of 'adult issues', though she

33

had heard the phrase often when she had asked her parents what they were fighting about. In Lucy's opinion, if she was old enough to notice, then she was old enough to get an answer about what the problem was. Unfortunately, that hadn't occurred to either of her parents.

This was her fourth house move, but the difference this time was that her Dad hadn't come with them. He was staying in their last house, but she was forced to move away from him to a tiny village next to a stupid lake. She didn't even like swimming.

Though she didn't yet know what it meant, Lucy had picked up on her Dad's pattern. He'd make a friend, someone from work usually, and then her Mum would get angry. Well, Lucy didn't know much about adult relationships, but she guessed that these friends of her Dad's must have been pretty awful because she was dragged to a new house every time her Mum found out about one of them. But for some reason, this time was different.

Her Mum was always the one who insisted on the move and she had always said they needed to do it to 'keep the family together'. Now, all of a sudden, Lucy's Dad wasn't welcome.

Lucy stood outside the front door of the new house with her arms crossed over her chest and that furrowed brow look she had learned from her mother. Julia struggled to lift a box, smiling at her daughter.

"Help your Mum out and hold the door open," Julia breathed, shuffling towards the house, whilst trying to keep the bottom of the box together. Lucy pursed her lips, her eyes flashing with defiance.

"I want to go home," she replied. She stared at the back of her Mum's head as she struggled past, willing it to explode.

"Lucy-Loo, we've been over this," Julia panted, kicking the door open herself and stumbling through it.

Lucy let her arms drop to her sides and swung them as she turned her attention away from the house and towards the lake. She crinkled her nose. As she surveyed the water and the surrounding trees, she felt a chill pass through her. How could her mother have not picked up on it when it was so apparent to her, an eleven year-old, that there was something wrong with the place?

Lucy shivered despite the clear sky and sun beaming down on her warm skin. She had that feeling that she was being watched, but couldn't see anyone peeking at her from the trees. She took a moment to try and settle her nerves, but that feeling of eyes on her wouldn't go away. She decided that maybe she would go inside the house after all.

* * *

Milky eyes watched the little blonde girl as she cast another uneasy look around and then vanished inside the lake house. Once the girl was completely out of sight, those eyes closed and sunk back underneath the lake water.

* * *

Lucy couldn't sleep that night; she hated her new house and she hated her new bed. She hated the tree that scratched on her window like icy fingers, and she hated the wind that was moving those branches in the first place.

Finally, at three o clock in the morning, Lucy decided that if she couldn't get to sleep then she might as well get up and do something productive. The sting of the move was still making her mind throb like it had been stroked with stinging nettles, but she had come to the conclusion that there was no point in whining about it. She had refused point blank to unpack any of her things in her new room, much to her mother's annoyance, and had gone to bed angry.

It was the powerlessness that was bothering her; she had been told they were moving and that was that. She'd not been asked about how she felt or at least where she'd like to live, it was just 'Lucy, pack your things'. She hadn't even been asked who she wanted to live with. Had she been given an option (and she thought she had a right to one), she would have stayed with her Dad.

A tear rolled over her cheek as she pulled back her bed covers and slid her feet into her bunny slippers. How was she supposed to live day-to-day, without her Dad there? She loved her Mum, but she was her Dad's girl. Her mother was the rule setter. There was no way she was going to get American pancakes for breakfast from her mother. She was going to have to complete jigsaws on her own from now on. Her weekends would no longer be for socialising with the friends she hoped to make in her new school. From now on, she'd been told in an oh-so-matter-of-fact fashion, she would be spending the weekends with her Dad. Only two lousy days a week with her favourite person on the planet, and no free time to even attempt to make other friends, and that's all folks.

Lucy looked around her dark bedroom, debating whether or not to turn on the light. It would be easier to find what she wanted if she did, but then her Mum was more likely to catch her out of bed. Unwilling to interact with Julia, she decided she would manage by moonlight.

She still had no plans to completely unpack her bedroom, but she would make an exception for the framed photograph of her Dad dressed as Father Christmas. She loved that picture, and she needed at least one element of her father in this strange, new room.

As quietly as possible, Lucy slid the curtains open, wincing as the old, metal hoops clinked together. She blinked against the silver light pouring into her room, waiting for her eyes to adjust. She took in her new view, and reluctantly acknowledged to herself that it was pretty spectacular, though she would never admit that to Julia.

She blinked again, but not because of the light. She stared at the surface of the lake, doubting her own instinct. That feeling that something was wrong crept back in, alerting her senses and causing the hairs on her arms to rise up. It took her a second, then the howl of the wind untangled her confusion about what *it* was.

The wind was kicking up dust and dirt from around the lake, and whipping the tree branches into a frenzy, but the lake was so still; it was as though it were frozen. Lucy's eyes searched for a ripple or a shimmer or any indication of movement. The water stared back at her, cold and motionless.

Lucy pressed her hands to the window and squished

her nose against the glass, trying to get a better look. The lake looked like a mirage, as though it wasn't of the same time as everything that surrounded it. It didn't belong.

hi

Alarmed, Lucy shrunk away from the glass. She had heard her name spoken loud and clear, though felt that she was the only one in the world that had the ability to hear it.

come play

Trembling, Lucy pressed her hands over her ears, trying to force the voice out. It was like her own mind had created the sound, but she knew better. She hesitated, and then returned to the window to investigate.

A small sound escaped her as she locked eyes on the girl in the lake. Visible from the chest up, the little girl smiled up at Lucy's window and waved. Lucy squinted at her. The girl must have been treading water because she was in the centre of the lake, though she didn't appear to be moving at all. There were still no ripples in the water, Lucy realised.

She raised her hand, wondering if she should wave back. It seemed a casual enough gesture, but she had the feeling that it would establish something between them. She wasn't sure that she wanted to be connected to the girl in the lake. She stood there for a while, her hand raised but unmoving, until the girl did something altogether unnatural.

The only way that Lucy could rationalise what she was seeing was to conclude that the lake must indeed be frozen solid on the surface, because the girl climbed atop it and sat with her legs tucked underneath her. The girl waved again and gestured for Lucy to come outside.

They stared at each other for a long while. Eventually, the girl leaned forward, pressed her hands to the surface of the lake, and then began to crawl across the water towards the house. Her dark hair fell at her shoulders, obscuring part of her features as she snaked along the lake like someone had hit the fast forward button.

Lucy stumbled backwards, yanking the curtains closed as she went. She clasped her hands to her mouth, breathing heavily, and darted towards one of her unpacked boxes. She had no idea which box the photo of her Dad was in, but she suddenly needed it. She tore through them all in a matter of minutes, flinging stuffed animals, books and board games out of her way. When she got to the bottom of the last box, she gritted her teeth and thumped the floor. It wasn't there and there was only one person who could have moved it.

On cue, Julia opened the door and peered into the darkness, irritated.

"Lucy, what on earth do you think you're doing?" Julia mumbled, feeling around the wall for the light switch. Both Lucy and Julia raised a hand to their eyes as the bare bulb illuminated the room. Julia's jaw became slack as she looked at Lucy's strewn clothes and belongings. Lucy forgot about everything else when she saw her mother's 'you're in so much trouble' expression. For once, she was more angry than concerned about whatever punishment her mother would dole out.

"Where is it?" Lucy demanded, standing up. Julia stared at her, raising her eyebrows. She had just walked in to her daughter's bedroom at past three in the morning, found it annihilated, and now she was getting attitude.

"Drop the scowl, young lady," Julia replied, using her warning tone. Lucy kicked the empty cardboard box in front of her and pointed at her mother.

"Give it back! Just because you hate Dad, it doesn't mean that I have to!" Lucy cried, all the nervous energy from the past few minutes manifesting into pain. "I need my photo!"

"Lucy, you had better calm down," Julia said in her most commanding tone, though she suddenly felt weak. "I'll get it for you."

Julia slipped out of the room and headed downstairs. Lucy didn't want to follow her so she stayed in her own room, stomping right over some of her strewn clothing. When her mother returned holding the stolen picture, Lucy felt like crying but managed to hold back the tears. Julia held the picture out to her, smiling. Lucy snatched it out of her hands, inspecting it for damage.

"I don't hate your father," Julia lied, standing in the doorway. She felt too unwelcome to fully enter the room. "I was afraid it would get broken amongst your games so I wrapped it up and put it in my handbag."

Lucy's features softened and she headed back towards her bed, the picture clutched to her chest like a safety blanket.

"I miss Dad," Lucy confessed, allowing her mother to see the vulnerability she'd been trying to hide. Julia hovered in the doorway for a moment then switched off the light.

"We'll talk about this in the morning," she replied, closing the door.

Lucy lay in bed clutching her picture for a long time, stewing on Julia's final sentence. She wasn't stupid; she knew full well what 'we'll talk later' meant. It was a phrase often used by her mother to avoid uncomfortable conversations or questions she didn't want to answer. In the morning when Lucy would attempt to bring up the subject of her Dad, her Mum would repeat the cursed phrase and that would be the end of it.

That was one of the things she missed the most about her Dad; he *listened* and he would answer her questions. Her mother just talked down to her and drank wine most of the time. Depending on whether Julia was on bottle number two or three, Lucy might get punished if she pushed an issue too much.

At about five in the morning, Lucy decided that she would run back home. It was a couple of hours to drive, so she figured she might be walking for a few days. She didn't care how long it would take; she just needed to get home.

She found her pink backpack amongst her strewn belongings, packed her photograph and a light jacket, and then tiptoed downstairs. She grinned when she saw the front door key sitting there in the lock, not believing how easy her escape was.

Once outside and full of defiant excitement, she set off along the footpath towards the canopy of trees that would eventually lead to the main road. The house was barely out of sight when she heard it —

don't go

Lucy froze, trying to will herself forward. Fear weighted her soles to the ground, and curiosity forced her to turn her head towards the lake. The girl sat cross-legged on the surface of the water, staring at Lucy with the saddest expression. Lucy recognised it as loneliness; she had seen it in the mirror a thousand times.

Lucy approached the water's edge, swallowed her fear, and waved. The girl waved back, beaming.

wait

The girl appeared to melt away into the water. Lucy scanned the lake, irritated by the girl's swift departure now that she had finally given in and responded. She was about to stomp off when the girl emerged at the water's edge just a foot away from where Lucy stood.

"Hi," Lucy said, gripping the straps of her backpack. The girl smiled.

"Hi!" the girl replied in an unearthly, ethereal chime. Lucy was taken aback; the voice came from the girl's mouth for sure, but it sounded like it also came out of the lake itself, and was tinged with a slight echo.

"What are you doing in there?" Lucy asked, moving a little closer. "It must be freezing?"

"I'm so hungry," the girl replied. Lucy stared at her, really taking in her appearance now that they were up close. Her hair hung heavily around her face, though it somehow wasn't wet, and her lips were frosted a greyish blue that matched her deathly pallor. What struck Lucy most were the girl's eyes; they were glazed with a milky film but still retained a hint of blue underneath. The girl looked about her age, Lucy figured, but those eyes said different.

Lucy, resigning herself to having to make her escape another time, held out her hand.

"Why don't you come in to my house? It's warm in there and we have food."

The girl smiled but shook her head. Lucy frowned, wondering why on earth not, and shrugged her backpack off her shoulders. She unzipped her bag, pulling out her jacket and held it out to the girl.

"You can have my jacket then," Lucy offered, shaking it in the girl's direction. The girl, smiling, reached for it but was just that bit too far. Lucy stepped to the very edge of the lake bank but then she started to slide. She lost her footing so quickly that for a second she couldn't understand why she was looking at the sky through a glass film. Then the coldness took her.

Lucy kicked against the water, confused about which way was up. Her throat and nose burned as she breathed in freezing water and her chest felt like it was collapsing in on itself. Her eyes stung but she forced them to stay open, searching for the right direction to kick in. Each passing second made it harder to move. A shape above her floated into view and she realised it was her backpack. She struggled up towards it, pain swelling in her chest with the need to breathe, and felt a tug on her ankle. She kicked, unable to free herself, and then looked down. Weeds snaked around her ankle, holding her in place. Everything started to go dark.

Lucy's eyes were closing when she felt something even colder than the water take hold around her waist, then she was heading up. She gasped, gulping in air that felt hot against how cold she had become.

Once safely on the lake bank, Lucy looked back at her savior. The girl hovered with her torso above the surface, the water perfectly still around her.

"We're friends now," the girl chimed.

Both of their heads turned towards the house as the porch light went on. Without a word, Lucy's new friend slipped under the surface as though she had never been there at all.

"Wait!" Lucy called. "What's your name?"

Alice

* * *

After her late-night escape attempt, Lucy had been in a lot of trouble and the tension with her mother had reached fever pitch. Lucy had explained that she couldn't sleep, went for a walk, and slipped. Of course this was a lie, but as far as she was concerned, her mother had no reason to doubt her. However, Julia hadn't bought the story and was instead convinced of an alternative explanation; she wholeheartedly believed that Lucy had planned to drown herself.

Lucy laughed at first, finding the accusation ludicrous. Why the hell would she actually try to do something like that? She couldn't wrap her mind around her mother's logic at all. Julia had cried, insisting that Lucy was trying to punish her for leaving her father, and grounded her for a month. Lucy wouldn't have minded so much if it had been during term time as she would have at least been away from the house for school, but being stuck indoors during the summer holidays was beginning to drive her stir crazy.

At least she had Alice. Although she couldn't go out to the lake, she could still talk to her through the windows. She didn't know how Alice managed to hear her, or be heard from the lake, but they shared a connection that made it possible.

Over the course of that month, Lucy told Alice all about her parents and how much she hated her mother. Alice was a good listener, and always had the right things to say. In all the moves, and all the schools, Lucy had never made a friend so easily.

On the last day of her punishment, Lucy decided that she would finally unpack properly and make her room her own. Now that she had a new best friend, she had reconsidered her reluctance to stay.

On her first day of freedom, Lucy went straight out to the lake. Julia forced her into a life jacket first, but Lucy didn't put up a fight; she figured she was lucky she was allowed to be near the water at all. Part of that, she hoped, was that Julia was learning to trust her. The reality, and she knew it, was just that Julia was beginning to care less about what she got up to. She was far more interested in the bottom of the bottle, and prattling on about what a scumbag Lucy's father was.

"Alice?" Lucy whispered, keeping her eye on the house for her nosey mother. She had walked to the far edge of the lake, hoping that from that distance, her mother wouldn't be able to see Alice. She wouldn't understand.

Alice emerged and clambered onto the surface of the water, lying across it with her eyes closed. Lucy grimaced and covered her nose with her hand.

"What's wrong with you?" she asked, her hand muffling her voice. Alice struggled to open her eyes. Her skin, though Lucy recognised it wasn't normal in the first place, looked weird. It was tinged in places with circular patches of greens and browns. The smell was unrecognisable to Lucy, which was understandable; she was totally unfamiliar with the stench of rotting meat.

"I'm hungry," Alice croaked, murky water spilling from her lips. Lucy looked at her friend, pained and conflicted. Her voice no longer chimed but sounded dull and flat.

"I don't think I can do it," Lucy muttered, guilt slapping her. Alice tipped her head in a nod of understanding.

They had discussed Alice's situation and her needs over the course of the month, and Lucy had promised to help. Now, faced with the prospect of having to come through on her promise, she wasn't sure she had the gall for it.

She sat with Alice for a while, who didn't move but tried to smile despite her disintegration. As the time went by, she started to float on top of the water, rather than resting on it in that otherworldly way that Lucy hadn't questioned. Instead of being one with the water, it now appeared that the lake was beginning to digest her.

Dirty water ran from Alice's eyes when the sun began to set, and Lucy felt her own fresh, clean tears run over her cheeks. She decided that though she had promised not to, she would have to tell her Mum about Alice. Grown ups knew how to deal with these things. Promising to return with help, Lucy made off towards her house. Alice was barely able to protest.

Lucy threw open the door and tracked dirt straight to the kitchen, where she could hear her mother talking on the phone.

"Mum, you have to come outside to the lake!" Lucy cried, full of the responsibility of keeping her only friend alive. Julia half-turned towards her and smiled.

"Yeah, I think so too, see you soon. Bye." Julia hung up the phone, beaming at her daughter as though she were Santa Claus with a sack full of presents. "Great news, Lucy-Loo!"

"Please, my friend is.."

"We're going home."

Lucy was rendered dumbfounded by her mother's declaration, then she was angry. Despite her pleading to stay at their own house, her mother had stripped the choice from her as callously as she ripped off plasters. Lucy hadn't been allowed to see her Dad all month because it was 'too painful' for her mother to come face to face with him, but now apparently everything was peachy.

Lucy thought about her perishing friend, the only company she had in this new, stupid house that she was just starting to like. She had finally unpacked her room. She was actually looking forward to starting yet another new school, where she would undoubtedly be picked on for being the new kid. Again.

She had a good friend, who listened to her woes and

reassured her. That friend wasn't going to make it without Lucy's help, and now her mother expected her to move again without asking how she felt about it. Her dearest mother had just gone right ahead and made the decision, without letting her know that there was even talk of a change of plans.

Well, Lucy decided, she wasn't leaving. Not this time and not just so they could spend another year or so as a family then have to up and move somewhere else. She was staying put, but she knew her mother would never see things her way.

She compared her seething temper, caused by her mother as usual, to the dismay of watching the best friend she'd ever had fizzling out like a match. The answer came so easily to her that she realised that she'd actually been willing for a while to do what Alice asked.

* * *

"It really is a lovely lake," Julia agreed, ambling around an unruly patch of weeds near the water's edge. Lucy tugged at her mother's hand.

"Come on, the best bit is over there!" she demanded, pointing at the area in which she had last seen Alice. Her friend was nowhere in sight, and Lucy felt a sickness rising inside her. She hoped she wasn't too late.

"Okay, okay!" Julia laughed, enjoying her daughter's excitement. It had been a long time since Lucy had smiled at her, and she was sure the news that they would be moving back in with her Dad was the cause of her sudden joy. When Lucy had suggested they take one last walk around the lake, Julia couldn't believe her luck. This type of invitation was normally only reserved for Lucy's Dad.

They finally reached the spot and Lucy let go of Julia's hand, edging towards the lake bank. She peered into the water for any sign of Alice, not knowing exactly how to proceed. Julia appeared at her side, looking into the water.

"Looking for something?" She smiled, stooping forward to try and get a better look. Julia tipped forward, resting her hands on her knees to keep her balance. Lucy smiled. Perfect.

"Don't you see it?" Lucy asked, noting a set of milky eyes rising to the surface.

"No, what am I looking for, honey?" Julia mumbled, now so near the edge that her toes were practically already in the water. Lucy slipped backwards a few feet and took a deep breath. Then she charged towards her mother with outstretched hands. Julia didn't even have time to scream as she went headfirst into the lake. She stumbled onto her knees, completely submerged until she jerked her head above the surface, gasping first with shock and then with anger.

"Lucy! What the hell do you think you're doing?" Julia bellowed, angrier than she had felt in a long time. Lucy ignored the question, walking towards the edge and searching for Alice. Julia, teeth gnashed together like she was trying to break them, stood up and rubbed her eyes. She had stumbled a few feet in and stood with the water up to her waist, her soaking dress clinging to her freezing body.

Lucy's heart sank as Julia waded towards her, yelling about how much trouble she was in. Then, just as Julia got to knee level in the water, she was yanked backwards by something from underneath. Julia fought against the pull and threw herself forwards with her arms out in front of her. Her expression questioned how Lucy could possibly be doing this. A moment later, she started screaming.

Alice burst through the surface of the lake with red running over her chin and down her throat. She clutched a piece of something in her hands as she gnawed on it. The way she ate reminded Lucy of one of those nature programs about wild animals feeding.

Julia stared at her daughter as the surface of the lake around her turned red. She dug her hands into the dirt of the lake bank and pulled herself forward, screaming for help. Lucy sat down in the grass and drew her knees up to her chest, watching what she had done. It was the first time she had ever felt in control of anything.

Alice finished with the chunk of flesh she was eating and dived on top of Julia, clawing the back of her dress to shreds. Once the material was out of the way, she brought both hands down in a scooping motion and tore a strip of skin right off Julia's spine. Julia howled.

It went on for a while.

It went on until only bones and the last bit of flesh in Alice's hands remained.

Lucy watched the whole thing.

* * *

Alice sat in her usual cross-legged position, chewing. She already looked healthy by comparison to how she looked just thirty minutes before.

50

"How come you changed your mind?" Alice asked, around a mouthful of muscle. Lucy eyed a chunk of her mother's floating hair, which was headed towards the middle of the lake.

"She was going to make me leave."

Alice swallowed the lump of meat in her throat and stopped chewing, wiping her chin with the back of her hand.

"What about when your Dad comes?"

"Why do you think he'll come here?" Lucy asked, furrowing her brows.

"He'll wonder where you are, won't he?" Alice replied, licking her lips. Lucy's eyes widened; that hadn't occurred to her. She probably only had a few days before her Dad would get worried enough to come looking, and then what would she do?

"Can't you come with us?" Lucy begged, knowing the answer. Alice smiled at her in that way that had developed when one of them asked a silly question. Lucy picked at the grass beside her. "How come you can't come out of the water?"

Alice let her hands fall into her lap, still clutching the piece of unrecognisable, gnarled flesh.

"This lake is special. Once it makes you, you stay," Alice explained. "If he had done it anywhere else, I don't think I would have come back."

"My Dad would never do that to me," Lucy replied, shaking her head. Alice shrugged, though more in sad reflection than disagreement.

"That's what I thought too, but when my Mum left he said it was my fault. He brought me out here and held my head under until I couldn't breathe any more."

Lucy's eyes shimmered with tears that she told herself were for her friend, though she suspected what had happened to her mother was now setting in. Alice looked over her shoulder at the house.

"I saw them arrest him, you know. Right there on the porch. He said I'd run away, but they saw the bite mark I left on him. Took a chunk right out of his hand as he held me under, but it did no good."

"I don't want to go away," Lucy mumbled, her lips trembling. Alice turned back towards her, a glimmer of something flashing across her face.

"You could stay. You could be like me," Alice's voice chimed along the wind. "I know how to do it."

"Like you?" Lucy considered, and then looked at her mother's floating hair again. Alice smiled, holding out her last chunk of meat.

"It's not so bad when you get used to it."

Lucy stood up and walked to the edge of the lake, staring at the flesh in Alice's hand. She grimaced.

"Stay here with me." Alice begged.

we can be best friends forever

Lucy dipped her toe into the lake and yanked it back out immediately. Alice read her thought.

"When you're like me, you won't feel the cold," she smiled, holding the flesh out again. Lucy stood there pondering over her options and then shook her head.

"I can't do it. I want my Dad," she said. Alice continued to smile, though her eyes betrayed her true feelings. Lucy turned and began to walk back to the house.

but I don't want to be alone any more please

"I'm sorry, Alice. Maybe I can convince him to live here instead."

please

"I'll visit you," Lucy assured her, fully intending on keeping the promise.

"Wait!" Alice pleaded, her voice loaded with the strain of tears. Lucy felt awful but she continued towards the house. They were best friends but they weren't the same.

"Don't you want this back?"

Lucy stopped and turned around. Alice still grasped her last bit of food in one hand, but there was now something rectangular in the other. Alice held it out to her, smiling.

"My picture!" Lucy squealed, darting back. She had thought that the photograph of her Dad was long gone because of the night she lost her backpack when she fell in the lake, but there it was in Alice's outstretched hand.

Alice extended the photograph. Lucy teetered at the edge, looking at Alice and questioning why she wasn't coming closer.

"I can't leave the water, remember?" Alice reminded her. Lucy waded in, shivering, and walked until everything but her head was submerged. Alice let the picture fall into the water and then she slithered towards Lucy.

In the instant it took for Lucy to realise how foolish

she'd been, Alice already had her free hand on the back of Lucy's head.

"Why did you save me before if you were going to do this anyway?" Lucy screamed, trying to wriggle out of Alice's grasp.

"It wouldn't have worked before. I didn't have anything to feed you then," Alice hissed, forcing the chunk of flesh into Lucy's mouth. Lucy screamed and fought, breathing in blood. A chunk of meat slipped down her throat, making her gag. Alice pressed her hand to Lucy's mouth, forcing the vomit back down as she held her head under the water.

* * *

Though things about Lucy changed, she didn't age any more, not on the outside. But the years taught her even more than Alice did. At first, she was angry and scared, but as she became one with her new setting, she felt a sense of empowerment creep in.

The disadvantage of not being able to leave the water was soon forgotten with the arrival of the skills she'd witnessed from Alice. Now one with the water, she moved as though she was part of it. What came after life, day to day with Alice, was a joy. They talked, they played, and they laughed. Things only became difficult when they were hungry.

Lucy had waited a long time for her Dad to arrive, but that day never came. She had planned how to explain everything to him, how to get his attention, and how to convince him to move to the house so they could be together every day. But her energy was wasted on plans that would never come to fruition. When she and her mother didn't show up to reunite with him, he had simply let her slip away. She remembered that every time she wished Alice hadn't changed her. Her bitterness turned into gratitude that though she had lost her parents, she had gained someone that would never – could never – leave.

They watched people come and go from the house; the owners never lasted long. Sometimes a single person would move there, which was best for Lucy and Alice because they made easier targets. Families tended to flee after one of their own was taken into the lake, but they were fun while they lasted.

* * *

Two pairs of milky eyes peered at the new, little boy through his bedroom window. He waved.

NOW
YOU
SEE
THEM

Now You See Them

Bobby slapped his hands over his eyes and came to a complete stop just outside his bedroom. Lisa looked down at her son and then peered into the gloom of his room.

"What's wrong, Bobby Bear?" she asked, tugging at her son's wrist. His elbow locked, his arm going rigid so that she couldn't pull his hand away from his face. "Bobby? Baby, open your eyes."

"They're in there!" Bobby hissed, his arm trembling in Lisa's hand. "If I look at them, they'll eat me up!"

Lisa smiled at her son's creativity and commitment to his intention; kids were forever inventing reasons not to go to bed. A few minutes later, Bobby was tucked in, under his mother's promise that his light would stay on all night. He swept the room with wide eyes, and then closed them. He breathed a sigh of relief, realising that through his eyelids he could see still see the glow of the bulb, and let himself drift off.

Three chimes of the grandfather clock downstairs yanked Bobby out of sleep and straight into the real nightmare. His body was tense and glazed with a sheen of sweat that glued his dinosaur pyjamas to him. He knew immediately what was wrong; his mother had lied to him. He couldn't see the glow through his eyelids, which could only mean that while he slept she had come back and turned out the light.

He kept his eyes squeezed shut, his heart hammering in the back of his throat and his ears. He pressed his lips together, trying to stop his breath from bursting out in the shotgun shudders he felt in his chest. Something, and Bobby knew it with every fibre of his being, was right above his face.

Despite himself, Bobby whimpered and then held his breath, panicked. He was only safe from the things in the dark if he was asleep, and he hoped that they thought he still was.

If he opened his eyes, if only a crack, he would see them. And then they'd be able to get him.

He'd been trying to tell his mother this for weeks, since he had first noticed one of them snaking towards him with liquid limbs from the corner of his eye. She said it was his eyes playing tricks in the dark, but it wasn't his eyes, it was *them*.

He held the sound of his sobs in, forcing them back down into the pit of his stomach, but it wasn't good enough. His torso jerked with stifled breath, rocking the mattress underneath him. The face hovering over his got closer, he could feel the warmth of its skin radiating onto him.

Bobby squeaked as something hot and dry brushed past his foot underneath the duvet. He pressed his lips together so hard that he bit them in an attempt to take back the sound he had just made. His mattress creaked, but not just in one place; there were at least six of them on his bed now.

Bobby's sobs turned into audible whimpers as tiny but sharp fingertips took a hold of his eyelashes and tugged his eyelids upwards. Bobby tensed everything, trying to keep his eyes shut. They'd get him if he saw them. They were trying to force him to look.

It was useless; his eyes opened just a crack. It was dark but he saw them. He saw the teeth.

Lisa bolted into her screeching son's bedroom, fumbling for the light. In the dark, she thought she saw a dozen separate shapes moving around Bobby's bed. She found the light and started screaming.

Bobby tumbled to the floor, his blood-covered hands feeling around as though he was still in the dark – and he was. He turned his face towards her, the hollow, weeping sockets where his eyes had been boring into her. She slid down the wall onto the floor, her mouth forming a silent 'O'.

"They ate them!" Bobby howled, with as much blame towards her as there was pain. "They ate them!"

Kayleigh Marie Edwards

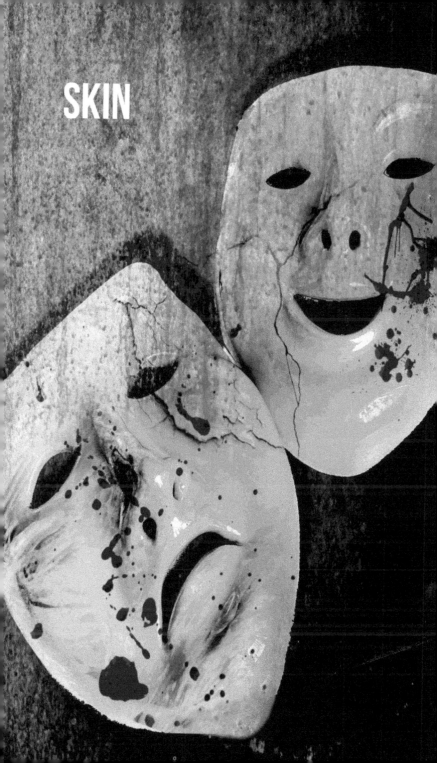

SKIN

Kayleigh Marie Edwards

Skin

It was a slow burn, but a hot one. Amy Cook winced as she pulled her hand back from her calf, which was already tender to the touch. She stared at the arachnid and shuddered as it crawled away. She wasn't the biggest fan of spiders and this particular one was behaving in an odd way; usually the little hell minions scuttled off, shying from the light that exposed them to bigger prey (which, in this instance, was most likely to be Amy's shoe). This spider, however, travelled with the nonchalance of one that had merely tipped his hat at her, rather than sinking its fangs into her flesh.

"Wait a minute, Ames," Martin insisted, putting himself between her and the beast before she could annihilate it.

"Nice to know whose side you're on," she mumbled, refocusing on her leg. It was a big spider, but even so, her wound was shocking. She could actually see the puncture wounds.

The bite was red and raw with a little blood oozing out. What concerned Amy though, was the yellow ring forming around it. The patch of skin that fell between the bite and the yellow ring had already turned a shade of grey, as though the spider had drained the life right out of the immediate area.

"Martin?"

"This is so weird," Martin replied, his attention completely devoted to the spider. He was on his hands and knees following it, as it strolled towards the nearest dark space – under the bed. "You should see the markings on this thing's back. I thought it was one of those false widows, but this pattern is more like a heart."

"If you let it run under my bed, I'm going to kill you!" Amy warned, panicked. Martin turned around in time for Amy's shoe to collide with the side of his face. He shot her a look that denied pain but expressed annoyance, before picking up the weapon and squashing his girlfriend's attacker.

"Happy?" he demanded, planning on giving her a mouthful about shoe-related abuse. "Ames?"

Martin turned again, ready to berate her. However, his girlfriend was unavailable for a telling off because she was unconscious.

* * *

Amy had managed to live her fifteen years without spending a day in the hospital. A night hooked up to monitors and drips had been no fun, and though she would never admit it to Martin, it was a little scary. He was teasing her for fainting as it was.

She was glad to be home, but the doctors hadn't exactly been reassuring. She propped herself onto her elbows, and shuffled up the bed, trying to find a comfortable sitting position. She still felt sick to her stomach, and a little light-headed.

Amy closed her eyes, heaved out a breath, and swung the duvet away from her leg. She opened her eyes, peering down at the wound, and immediately wished she hadn't. The yellow ring had turned a shade of gold with little blotches of green spreading through it. The pattern reminded her of marble, if marble were an organic, rotting substance. The patch between the yellow ring and the bite had turned china white and it throbbed with her pulse. The whole area was swollen and was beginning to give off a faint odour.

An allergic reaction to the spider's venom, probably a false widow, they had said. She had even been scolded for not catching the beast for analysis.

'Inconclusive' was the word they had used that had bothered her, and they had used it a lot. Two sets of blood tests were done, and both came back 'inconclusive'. The doctors blamed the new hematologist for the confusion, but for just a second, Amy had caught the look of perplexity on the doctor's faces. They took more blood and some urine, and sent her home to rest.

They didn't really think the hematologist had messed up, and neither did she. There was something *wrong* with that spider, and now there was something wrong with her too. She could feel it in her gut. Her stomach lurched suddenly.

She twisted out of bed, feeling sick, and pressed her hand to her mouth, wincing as her feet hit the ground. Her whole leg was sensitive to the touch, right down to her foot. She'd have to suffer and run anyway or she would throw up on her brand new bedroom carpet.

Ten minutes later, Amy was back in bed with tears trickling from her eyes. She tried not to think of her mother – who had abandoned her years before – but when she was unwell she just couldn't help it. Her dad tried, but he didn't have the right touch. He was too abrupt, and as someone who never fell ill himself, lost patience quickly. Her mum had left them when Amy hit her teens, and she resented her for it. Who was she supposed to go to with questions or problems? Puberty was stressful enough *with* a woman in the house, but it was a nightmare without.

A knock on her bedroom door suddenly brought her back to the land of consciousness. She hadn't even realised she'd dozed off. The door creaked open, and Martin strode in, grinning.

"How's it going, puke breath?"

Amy gritted her teeth. Whenever Martin came over, her dad would suddenly 'misplace' any pictures of her looking pretty, especially the holiday pictures of her by the pool. Yet, he never failed to mention it if she had happened to vomit, burp, or break wind that day.

"I feel a bit better," Amy lied. Martin left the door ajar and approached the bed, jumping into a cross-legged position at the bottom. He opened his backpack, rummaging through the contents.

"Miss Prosser gave me your homework."

"Great," Amy smiled. She wasn't so fond of the homework, but she was fond of Martin in his shirt and tie. He always wore it a bit loose just to spite the school uniform rules. He'd been in detention many times, though as far as Amy's dad knew, Martin was a model student. He was even part of the band, Amy had beamed. That had lightened the mood a little; Amy's dad was also in the school orchestra back in his day, once a keen violinist. Martin wasn't in the orchestra, he played guitar in a band with his friends, but Amy accidentally on purpose forgot to correct her dad's assumption. He only just tolerated Martin as it was.

"Ames?"

"Hmm?" Amy opened her eyes, embarrassed that she had drifted off again.

"I said, when are you back in school?"

"Couple of days," she lied again. She was feeling worse by the second. Martin tutted and rolled his eyes.

"You're making quite a big fuss, it's just a spider bite! Can I see it?"

Amy clenched the duvet, yanking it up to her chin. Martin's eyes shifted to the edge of the blanket where her legs were, but before he could snatch away her cover, Amy's dad entered the room.

"We're out of milk," he declared, his eyes fixed on Martin. Amy's face dropped – milk was the only thing she could stomach, which was odd, because normally when she felt sick, milk was the last thing she wanted. "Martin, would you mind popping to the shop? I don't want to leave Amy on her own right now."

"Can't you go? Martin can stay here with me," Amy rushed to ask, before Martin could refuse and show himself up as rude. Her dad's eyes shifted back and forth between them.

"I'm not leaving you two on your own."

"Thanks a lot," she mumbled, glaring at him. Martin continued to rummage through his bag, averting his eyes from both of them. Her dad sighed and mimicked her folded arm pose.

"What's the mood face for, Amy?"

"Nothing. Nice to know you trust me, that's all. You'll only be gone a minute, I don't know what you think we're gonna do."

She shot Martin a look as she spoke that warned him not to smirk, but he couldn't help himself and lowered his head into his bag to hide it from her dad. She coughed, hoping her dad hadn't caught the glint in Martin's eye. He unfolded his arms and shifted his weight on his feet, before finally lowering his gaze.

"I suppose. Martin?"

Martin lifted his head, the colour draining from his face. He pretended he wasn't, but he was a bit afraid of Amy's dad. He shot Martin his 'any funny business and I'll kill you' smile.

"I'll be back in two minutes, maximum."

Martin nodded, returning his smile with a nervous, tight-lipped smile of his own. Amy's dad stared at them both for a moment, and then left, making sure he nudged the door all the way open before he descended the stairs.

As soon as they heard the front door close, Martin turned to Amy with a suggestive grin.

"We can't!" Amy snapped, her fingers tightening on her duvet. Martin shrugged.

"You said you felt better just now!" Martin insisted, shuffling up the bed towards her. Amy smiled but Martin caught the blatant refusal in her eyes before she could argue her case further. He stood, yanking a book out of his bag, and tossed it onto her legs.

"Ow!" Amy reached down and pressed a hand to her leg, crying out as searing pain set her skin on fire. She yanked her hand back, composed herself, and then lifted the book off her injured limb.

"Read the first three chapters," Martin told her, pulling his backpack onto his shoulders and making for the door. His voice had turned from playful to cold, just like it always did when he didn't get his way. "You know, you're boring sometimes. We've already done it so I don't know what your problem is."

Amy felt the panic rise in her chest – she was ill and her boyfriend was about to leave her alone, but that really wasn't the cause of the lump travelling up her throat. She had upset him... again.

* * *

Martin had approached her at lunch about five months before. At first, Amy thought it was a joke. He was a popular boy *and* he was in the year above her. He had his pick of the girls, and he had made his way through quite a few of them. Amy had always daydreamed about him, as had everyone else. She had always defended him against the trail of heartbroken girls he left in his wake, insisting that when he found the right girl, he'd stick around.

She couldn't believe her luck when he started sitting with her every day at dinnertime. She knew she was no model, and she'd never had a boyfriend before. She was the bookworm type, sometimes she had to wear glasses; she definitely wasn't like the girls Martin normally went for. The other girls thought she was weird because her idea of fun was a good read, and she really didn't have any friends. And yet, there he was, joining her at every given opportunity.

Once she had accepted that he really did like her, they had become inseparable. He told her she was pretty a lot, and she was beyond flattered. He was the first male in her life ever to pay her a compliment, and before she knew what was happening she had got completely carried away. Her dad had resisted, but she persevered – she and Martin were meant for each other, and nothing would stand in the way.

She had always promised herself, and her dad, that she would wait until she was in love before she gave her virginity to someone. Her dad had actually been pushing for her to wait until marriage, but Amy didn't think that was very modern. Plus her dad would never have to know. They had done it at Martin's house after school before his mum got home from work. It had hurt like hell, and it had happened within the first month of their relationship. Amy would have preferred to wait, but Martin had seemed upset. Didn't she love him?

Afterwards, Amy wasn't sure that she wanted to do it again, but since they already had, she didn't see a logical reason to refuse him. Plus, there were a million other girls just waiting for Martin to realise that she wasn't good enough for him, all of whom were probably more than willing. So she had done it again. It didn't hurt as much as the first time, but it wasn't like the movies either. She hadn't felt good about herself for it, not one bit. She still didn't. She told Martin she wasn't ready to do it again for a while, but he didn't seem to understand.

"Martin, my dad said someone needs to stay…"

"He'll be back any minute anyway," Martin interrupted, nudging the door with his foot. Amy felt the stab of rejection in her chest, and the tense lump inched a little further up her throat. If she didn't get over whatever the hell her problem was soon, he was going to ditch her. Suddenly, she realised that the lump in her throat wasn't just the tears that she was choking on. Martin left just seconds before she threw up over the side of her bed.

* * *

Sleep came whenever it pleased for the next twelve hours. She cried into her pillow, frustrated with herself for upsetting Martin, who hadn't called. One minute, she was so tired and angry about her inability to sleep that she grit her teeth hard enough to send pain into her gums, and the next, she was waking up from a feverish red haze.

Around four in the morning, she awoke from a nightmare, the details of which she could not recall. Yet, senses lingered; a white hot burn, like she were aflame, and a rancid smell. As her eyes adjusted to her dark bedroom, she realised those dream sensations were not only lingering but intensifying. Her leg felt like it was bathed in acid.

She knocked her glasses off the nightstand as she fumbled for the lamp. She eventually found it after scattering plastic jewellery and her schoolbooks onto the floor, and pressed her hand to her eyes as light illuminated the room. It cast away some of the darkness, but none of the pain. She shuffled into a slouched position, trying to hold in her screams for fear of waking her dad up, and looked down at the shape of her leg. A dark, wet patch had spread all the way through the duvet. She closed her eyes, counted to three in her head, and tore the blanket away.

She couldn't hold in the scream this time. Her flesh, which was stuck fast to the fabric, tore away with the duvet as she threw it back. Blood seeped from her shredded leg in some places, and spurted from one area, where the most skin and tissue had come away. Instinctively she reached down and pressed both hands to it, cursing herself as her limb exploded with pain. She stared, wide eyed despite the light, at the raw wound. About a third of the flesh on her shin was now stuck to the blanket, torn completely away. As her heart quickened, she thought she could see her pulse dancing in the blood and puss that trickled out.

Her bedroom door opened violently enough to hit the wall, as her dad hit the light switch on with the palm of his hand and then raced towards her, first angry, then almost as horrified as she was. He stopped in his tracks, his mouth hanging open. Amy looked at him, and then followed his gaze back to her leg, which, under the main light looked far worse. Not only had a huge chunk of her flesh peeled away, but her leg was now porcelain white from her toes to just above the knee. It didn't look human.

Amy realised her cheeks were wet, but couldn't make sense of the reason, though she could hear herself crying in machine-gun sobs. She looked at her dad, who was staring at her blood-covered hands.

"Amy…" his voice was soft, for the first time in her life. "Why would you do this to yourself?"

* * *

It had been a long and painful night for both of them. It had taken her a while to convince him not to take her to the hospital; she was terrified, and the last place she wanted to be was in an unfamiliar bed surrounded by sick people. She had thought for sure he was going to force her into the car, so she had resorted to the one line she knew he could never fight against – *mum wouldn't force me to do this.*

Two hours later, she was back in bed on top of fresh sheets. Her dad had found some anti-septic lotion in the back of the bathroom cabinet, and had cleaned her leg and wrapped it in a bandage. The process had been agonising, and she couldn't watch. She focused on her dad's face instead, though his expression seemed to mimic her agony. As grateful as she was for his help, she was angry. He said he believed her, though she knew he didn't. He couldn't lie to save his life. He actually thought that she had pulled her own skin off.

She was alone, her only company the lamplight, but she retained her irritated, folded-arm posture. She couldn't believe that her dad thought she would mutilate her own body. He didn't know her at all. Not like her mum had. She looked at the ceiling, trying to suck the tears back into her glistening eyeballs. She would not cry another tear over her mum.

* * *

Martin dropped the math book onto the nightstand, avoiding eye contact with Amy. The episode the night before now felt so unbelievable that if it weren't for the raw pain of her bandaged leg, she might have believed she dreamt it.

She smiled at Martin, reaching for his hand. She managed to brush his fingers before he moved to the bottom of her bed, sat down on the edge, and started scrolling through his phone. Her heart sank and accelerated simultaneously.

"Dad said you can stay for dinner tonight, if you want?" she tried, hoping for even a hint of his interest. It was the first dinner invitation Martin had ever received from her dad. Come to think of it, it was the first time her dad was going to actually cook a dinner that didn't involve the microwave. He must be really worried about her, Amy figured. Martin didn't look up.

"I don't know why the teachers keep giving me your homework to bring over."

"Because you're my boyfriend?" Amy responded, scolding herself for allowing the statement to come out as a question. Her eyes danced over his face, his crumpled shirt, and his loose tie. The mere sight of him made her smile, despite the glaring truth that his feelings for her were rapidly vanishing. Her eyes lingered on his tie, and then his neck. There was a round, red, blotchy mark on his skin. It looked like a bruise on first glance, but she knew it wasn't. Tears stung her eyes. The house phone rang in the background, but she barely acknowledged the sound, it was like she was drowning in suspended time.

"Yeah well, I'm not your slave. Get one of your friends to bring it next time," Martin sighed, finally making eye contact. His face flashed with cruelty as Amy's face crumpled. "Oh yeah, that's right. You don't really have any."

The pain in her leg suddenly felt like it was attacking her chest, her heart.

"Why are you being so mean?"

But she knew why. Martin's phone vibrated, and his eyes shifted back to it. He had intentionally made a dig, and it was nothing to him. He was talking to her like he talked to the nerds in his year that he and his friends thought were losers. Amy stared at him as he read his text, fighting to stop her lower lip from trembling as she watched the side of his mouth turn upward. She knew that look. It was a girl, probably the same one who had left the mark on his neck.

"Look, we both know this ain't working out, Ames. I think we should leave it."

Time stopped for her then. She was so angry with herself – she *knew* this would happen. She should never have been stupid enough to believe he liked her in the first place, to actually believe him. She should never have been stupid enough to let him… when she wasn't ready.

The anger left her as quickly as it arrived, then the devastation set in. She had known, realistically, that she was never good enough for him anyway, but though he was being mean, she didn't want to believe he didn't want her.

"You said you loved me," she whispered, cringing at how pathetic she sounded. Martin continued to stare at his phone, his thumb hovering over the keys as he responded to his text message.

"Yeah well, that was before you strung me along. I thought you were different, Ames."

"I… different to what?"

"I just didn't think you were one of those girls who dangles it in a guy's face and then turns him down. Get a kick out of winding me up, don't you." It wasn't even a question; he had made his mind up about her.

"No… I…"

Amy pulled the duvet to her chin, as though her blanket cocoon would stop her from shattering like frosted glass. Before she could humiliate herself further, footsteps pounded up the stairs. Her dad burst into the room, still clutching the cordless phone. His face was red, his eyes glassy. It reminded her of that red haze from her dreams. He strode across the room and gripped Martin by his collar, lifting him off her bed, and spun him towards the door.

"You little shit! I knew it!"

Martin's face twisted with terror as he was flung to the ground like a ragdoll. Amy's dad glared at him and pointed towards the door.

"Get out of my house! You ever come sniffing around my daughter again and I'll fucking kill you!"

Martin didn't need to be told twice; he bolted. Amy's dad turned towards her, the glaze in his eyes turning to tears.

"Why didn't you tell me?"

"Tell you what?" Amy brought her good leg up to her chest, feeling that she needed the defence.

"I knew it. I bloody knew it." He dropped his head into his hands and paced back and forth. "Jesus Christ Amy, I thought I raised you better than this. Why didn't you come to me with this instead of letting me hear it from some doctor at the hospital? This all makes sense now. I should have known when you started throwing up."

Amy's breath caught in her throat as the penny dropped.

"And don't try to tell me you didn't know you were pregnant Amy, or I swear to God…"

The sobs exploded from within her, painful enough even to numb the pain in her leg. She howled into her hands as everything around her crumbled to ash. She hadn't known. She hadn't even missed a period. She had been stupid enough to sleep with Martin, and she had been stupid enough to listen to him when he insisted he didn't want to use protection. But even in that moment, she wasn't too stupid to realise that she was almost halfway into her pregnancy.

* * *

Convinced that she had mutilated her own leg due to the stress of her 'secret', Amy's dad went full baby sitter on her. She was grounded, probably for life, she reckoned, and the next week was a nightmare. There was either something wrong with the pregnancy, or there was something wrong with her *as well as* the pregnancy. The real problem for Amy was her dad just wouldn't listen.

They had never been close, in fact, he had often been cruel, and even occasionally physical with her when she disobeyed or angered him. Even so, his disappointment sliced into her every time they were in the same room together. He simply couldn't look at her, and talking, other than to give her instructions, was out of the question. After the initial shock, and the tirade of abuse from him were over, he had gone mute. Days and nights passed by in an awkward, stilted fashion, and Amy felt truly alone. She would have preferred him to yell, but silence, as she knew her dad had worked out over the years, was really the best way to hurt her. She didn't feel, even in her current state, that her pain was worth his acknowledgement or attention, and he knew it.

Her dad would probably never forgive her for 'shaming the family' and she wasn't allowed to talk to him. With an already broken heart, she had tried to explain that Martin was the only one, but her dad had already come to the conclusion that she had been off 'gallivanting', and that once the secret was out she'd be known as the town bike. He was keeping her home from school until he could figure out 'what to do' about the baby, and she was under strict orders not to tell anyone what was going on. Even if she were allowed to go to school, she was too ill to go anyway. The burn in her leg had spread to her hip, and her entire body had adopted the porcelain hue. Her dad assumed it was the pregnancy making her pale and wouldn't listen to her arguments – he thought she was trying to detract from the real disaster.

Martin had been right with his snide comment about her lack of friends — she hadn't received a call or a visitor, and didn't expect to. Martin was the only thing she could think about besides her physical and emotional pain, and he wasn't exactly a comforting thought. She doubted he knew what the hell her dad had gone crazy on him for, and she was glad. Had he known about the baby, he probably would have ditched her earlier.

She was fifteen, motherless, and pregnant. She was in agony, she was sick, and she was terrified. She didn't even know what to be more scared of — the sickness spreading from the leg wound, or what she considered to be the sickness inside her womb. The only thing she knew was that she was completely and utterly alone.

* * *

Fire...

Amy, in her sleep, crunched her teeth together, but a whimper still escaped. Her eyes fluttered open, the pupils so big her eyes looked almost entirely black.

Pain...

Sweat matted her hair to her face, and her nightdress to her body. She was soaking wet, and for a moment she was convinced that she had been set alight. A gurgle escaped her throat as she tried to call out for her dad. She tried to move, but she couldn't. She was wide-awake, but the red haze of her nightmares hovered in her vision instead of dissipating like normal.

She lifted an arm, reaching for her lamp, and screamed, but the sound caught in her throat. Memories of the night the flesh tore away from her leg returned as she realised why she couldn't move – her entire body was stuck to the sheets, just like her leg had been. The sweat coating her body was unusually warm, and she croaked again as she recognised the velvet texture of the liquid not as sweat, but blood. She didn't need the light to know that the skin from her arm was no longer attached to her, at least not for the most part.

She tried to scream again, hoping to a god that she didn't believe in that her dad would just so happen to check on her at any moment. Hot tears streamed from her eyes, the salt stinging the layer underneath the skin as the moisture trickled through her bloody cheeks. Every sensitive and inflamed inch of her skin was coming away from her body, exposing the nerves and the red raw layer underneath, and there was nothing she could do to stop it.

Shedding....

She lay there in the dark, becoming grateful that she wasn't able to turn on the lamp after all. She didn't want to see what was happening. She tried to remain motionless, but every now and then, the pain would barrel through her, pitching, and an involuntary spasm would seize her. Every time it happened, a piece of her came away, matted to the sheets.

Hers weren't the only sheets she had lost a part of herself in. In the quieter moments where searing torture dulled to mere agony, she cast her mind back to that first night with Martin and wished she could take it back. This was her punishment. Her dad was right – she was a slut. Her mother was right – she wasn't worth sticking around for. Despite her 'A' grades, her domestic capabilities, and her wonderful manners, she was no longer a good girl. She had ruined it, and she could never be what she was again. She had changed, but into something worse than she had been before; she was somehow smaller. It was the worst kind of metamorphosis.

By now, the whole school would know that she was just one of many girls who had been used and disregarded; Martin had a habit of spilling the dirty details once he was done with a conquest, and despite her better judgment, she had allowed herself to join those shameful ranks.

Make it stop…

Please, make it stop…

Time lost all meaning as she lay there burning. Eventually, sunlight filtered through her curtains, and as the light grew, her pain seemed to lessen. Her radio came on automatically at eight, signaling her usual time to get up for school. She turned her head to look at it, and noticed that the movement didn't hurt so much. She closed her eyes, took a deep breath, and sat up. She screamed inside, but managed to keep her mouth shut, and then in one swift movement, swung her legs over the edge of her bed.

She rested a moment to compose herself as pain shuddered through her limbs and torso. After the wave had passed, she stood and, with stilted steps, made her way over to her full-length mirror. She looked at her reflection. She really had changed. She took in the new layer of skin, fancying that it was thicker and more durable than the last, though it was still raw, with small areas pumping out blood in little pools. Some of the old skin still clung on in places, but that would drop off. She tilted her head, examining the skull, noticing a clump of hair had fallen away along with the flesh.

She winced, taking a step back, and stared into her own eyes, both black, as numbness crept in. She would never be the same again. She smiled at her reflection as she realised that, and rested her hands on her hips. If nothing else, she certainly wouldn't blend into the background anymore.

She thought back to the day the spider bit her, which now felt like it was years ago, and smiled. All that pain was just a dull throb now.

She continued to smile at her own reflection as her dad entered the room, completely unaware of his presence. She was also unaware of the warmth trickling out of her wounds, carried in her blood.

Amy's dad stood in the doorway, silent as usual, but for a different reason. He looked at his once beautiful daughter, a picture of gore in her nightdress, bloody open scissors clutched in one skinned hand. A million thoughts raced through his mind but it seemed that there were none at all. Reason and logic had deserted him. Rooted to the spot, he marveled that his mutilated daughter had even survived the attack on herself, let alone that she was able to stand.

Finally alerted to his presence by his shallow sobbing, she turned towards him. He collapsed to his knees in shame, guilt, and mourning. He didn't know who was looking at him, but he was sure that his daughter was dead.

Amy clenched her fists, feeling an obstruction in one of them. She looked down, noticing the scissors, and raised them to eye level. She didn't remember picking them up, yet she felt their impression in her palm and realised she had been clutching them for a long time. Strands of gnarled flesh clung to the points.

'S' DAY

Kayleigh Marie Edwards

'S' Day

Picture, if you will, a little sod. Everyone knows one; some of you might even have one. Hell, I bet a couple of you were right little sods yourselves. Now, imagine that you are the parent of said little sod, and he's playing up. He's been noisy in the supermarket; he's thrown his toy on the floor. He ate straight from the pick'n'mix display and now you have to pay for sweets you didn't even let him have. Oh great, now he's full of sugar too.

That little sod has, say, two siblings, and they're starting to pick up on his behaviour. Oh no, you say to yourself, one of them is bad enough. Sometimes, though you'll deny this to everyone, you question why you had him in the first place. You'll be damned if his siblings become little sods too. So what do you do? You punish the lot of them, right? That makes sense – by punishing the innocent children, you ensure that they will become the enforcers of your rules. Little Sod's reign of terror is over if he ever wants his siblings to talk to him again.

Kate Taylor, a very lovely thirty-something year old, had one of those little sods. His name was Bobby, and I hated his eight-year-old guts. He was one of those kids that just had to be heard. All. The Time. They could hear him on earth and we could hear him in the damn, blasted heavens too. His shrill little voice was always demanding something, and Kate always caved. That would cease the torrent of verbal stabbings to our eardrums, if only for a while.

Well, one day, Kate decided that enough was enough. She wasn't going to feel guilty about being a single parent with a single income any more. Bobby needed discipline. And that's how it all started really. He made a request, nay, a demand, and she refused him. This was the starting point for what's known on Earth as 'S' Day. Planet dwellers think the 'S' stands for 'Soup', but we think it stands for 'Sod'.

On that fateful day, I was lying in a cloud with my hands clasped over my ears, wondering why God had created Bobby Taylor in the first place. Not that I'm one to question the Lord but I think if He were being honest, He'd admit that Bobby Taylor was a mistake.

You see, kids have a system; when they want something, they ask a parent. When that parent refuses, they go to the other parent, then their most gullible grandparent. If neither the second parent nor the grandparent options are available, they turn to Santa. But what if it's not Christmas, I hear you ask? Well, in that case, they start praying. And why wouldn't they? They're taught that God hears all their prayers, that He loves all of his children, and that He performs miracles.

When Kate refused Bobby's request for chicken soup (out of principle, it wasn't even lunch time), he bypassed all other routes and went straight for the Big Guy. And I'll tell you this for nothing now, whether He wants to or not, it's true that He does indeed hear every prayer. Every single one of them. So anyway, Bobby started praying. Relentlessly.

God was having a bad day at the office; it was a classic case of too many prayers and not enough time; there was a war that was... well, mid-war; some terrible virus was making the rounds; the Big Brother final was coming up (and that's always a busy one).

So you can imagine how annoying Bobby's steady stream of requests became. They were coming in fast and loud, interrupting other prayers, putting God off His train of thought, and generally causing a nuisance.

God tried to mute him, but it was no good; Bobby was determined to be heard. He was a loud kid in general, but when he wanted something, man, he could be persistent. We could all hear him way up in the clouds:

'Dear God, I really love chicken soup, please send me a life time's supply.'
'Dear God, I'm hungry for chicken soup.'
'God, why aren't you answering me?'
'G, where my soup at?'
'Oh Gooooddddd, I know you can heeeeeear meeeeee.'
And then the kicker;
'Dear God, if you loved me, you'd send me the soup I asked for.'

I took one look at God's face and knew that the planet was doomed. Ten plagues aside, God can normally control his temper. You wouldn't believe how often He hears 'If you love me then you'll…' It drives him absolutely bonkers.

'That little sod,' God said, massaging his temples. 'If he wants chicken soup, I'll give him chicken soup!'

And so it rained.

At first, Bobby was pretty excited when he felt the warm splash from above on his skin. He got more excited still when he licked it off his arm and declared that it was raining his favourite canned food. But then it poured, and it poured just on Bobby. Gallons of the stuff.

The kid tried to run, but you try running across chicken soup covered ground. It got real slippery real fast, and the next thing he knew, Bobby was arse over tit in a considerably sized puddle of creamy goodness. Then came the lumps of chicken - lumps the size of which you've never seen. All right, they weren't lumps. They were whole chickens. Frozen ones.

You can imagine what frozen chickens falling from the sky can do to a skull. Especially when, technically speaking, they're not falling, but rather being thrown like javelins from the arm of the Almighty.

That was the end of Bobby Taylor and it would have been the end of the whole episode if Kate Taylor had just kept her trap shut. God had had His fun, He'd vented some frustration, and He'd rid the world of the biggest little sod there was.

I'm sure you can sympathise with the Holy One when I tell you that Kate Taylor kicked off. I know what you're thinking - most parents would, right? She made this big fuss in front of the spectators who'd witnessed the chicken-skull fiasco. She claimed that Bobby was taken before his time, that God was an unfair so-and-so, and that she was turning her back on Him forever. I suppose any parent would, but the thing was, when God oh-so-literally answered Bobby's prayer, He was answering Kate's too.

Throughout the whole time we could hear Bobby rambling about his soup, we could also hear a very faint but persistent pleading cry for help from Kate. I'm sure, looking back on it now, that she actually used the phrase 'just kill the little fu...'... well, you can fill in the rest. As soon as she saw those chickens come down, she smiled. We all saw it. And then she had the gall to stand there wailing that it was a tragedy. Well, that really tied God in a knot. So He kept raining soup and He kept throwing chickens.

Remember that parent I mentioned earlier, the one who punishes all of their children for the crimes of one? Yeah, so that's what happened. Bobby lit the match, Kate dropped it on the kindling, and then God lost it for a minute and poured on the gasoline. For forty days and nights, the people of Earth endured warm soup floods, and frozen chicken related deaths.

When the puddles started to coalesce into lakes, we tried to stop Him, but He was in no mood to be told what to do. He had had it with the trivial prayers, expectations, and complaints from His Children. I tried to tell Him that they had learned their lesson, and that perhaps flooding the world with soup was a little overboard (da da dum). His reply was that in order to prove that He loves his children equally, He has to treat them all the same. If one needs a good smiting, then they all do.

The results of the flood were pretty bad for the majority. As you can imagine, due to the lack of warning, there was no time to build an ark. There wasn't even enough time to assemble a raft, though a few did manage to blow up some inflatables.

That's not to say that there weren't any survivors, though if you want to be technical about it, 'S' Day was what is considered a cull. Humanity has taken a somewhat bizarre turn since then. In a thousand years or so, I can't wait to see what future humans make of the cave drawings of those falling chickens.

Bobby, the absolute sod, has gone down in history as a martyr. Yeah, we couldn't believe it either.

With each of God's lessons, humanity takes something valuable away to progress with, but in this case they were left a little perplexed. Scholars continue to try to make sense of 'S' Day, but the only conclusion drawn so far is that chicken soup is now banned. I'm hoping that the next little sod prays for carrots; I can't stand carrots.

BARRY'S LAST DAY

Kayleigh Marie Edwards

Barry's Last Day

Barry Pufton had all kinds of troubles and he was just about sick to death of them. Up in plenty of time for work, as usual, Barry poured his second cup of coffee and thought about his life. He frowned.

Today was the day he was retiring from his job (which had always been just that; it had never blossomed into the career he'd hoped for), and he supposed that he should be feeling that lovely onset of earned satisfaction any minute now. There was only one thing delaying what he believed was his well-deserved R&R, and that was everything.

He'd hoped to retire not as the builder he'd been for forty odd years, but as a foreman. Just a few months earlier, he'd apparently been first in line for that promotion. That was until Todd Tafwell, the twenty-something year-old little shit, swanned in out of nowhere and impressed the site manager with his construction degree and his stupid Kim Kardashian jokes.

Barry didn't know what a 'Kardashian' was, and he didn't know what kind of stupid name Todd was either. They were British, for crying out loud. The kid had an education, as he often loved to point out, but he didn't know the first thing about a building site.

Barry narrowed his eyes as he sipped his coffee and then reached under the sink for his blue thermos. He glared at it, reminded of Todd. Everything reminded him of Todd these days, his thermos especially. As well as having barely any practical experience, Tafwell didn't seem to have any individual thought either. He'd arrived on his first day with a green thermos, then on the second day he'd turned up with a blue one. That wasn't a coincidence, Barry had decided. The kid had copied him, just to piss him off. *Hey look, I got your promotion, and now I've got your thermos too!*

He should have been glad to retire; years of shifting bricks had given him a sore back and rough hands, and he'd got to the point of having to make a noise when he got out of his chair. That Tafwell twat was the final nail in the coffin. The downside of course, was that once he was no longer in work, he'd have lots more time with his family.

His frown lines deepened as he considered that. More time with his insufferable wife, Gladys, and his disappointing son, Phillip, was the last thing he needed at his age. The only 'glad' thing about Gladys was the first four letters of her name. Barry often thought of other four-lettered names to call her.

And don't get me started on Phillip, Barry thought, pouring hot water into his thermos. Back in the day, he'd thought having a son was great. That was until Phil learned how to walk and talk and then it was all downhill from there. Apparently, walking and talking was all Phil had ever learned to do, because he still lived with his parents, despite being in his mid-thirties. And talking, if Barry were being honest, was a stretch for Phil, thanks to his drug habit.

Phil, since he'd hit his teens, was adamant that 'if it comes from the ground, it's not drugs', but marijuana and certain mushrooms were drugs in Barry's book. Barry eyed the small, plastic bag of mushrooms that he'd confiscated just the night before. He was surprised they were still on the kitchen counter where he'd left them – normally Phil would have stolen them back by now. At seven in the morning though, Phil was only likely to have switched his stupid games console off and gone to bed an hour ago.

"Barry, are you still here?" Gladys screeched, from upstairs. Barry felt the low wave of revulsion that he got every time he heard his wife's voice, and gathered up his lunch as quickly as he could move. He was normally long gone before she darkened his day by waking up, but recently she'd got into the annoying habit of 'seeing him off for work'.

That hour and a half in the morning before work was the only time he'd really had to himself for their entire marriage, especially since she'd given up her part-time hairdressing job to stay home and 'housewife', whatever that meant. Barry could only conclude that, like Todd, Gladys was just trying to ruin the little peace he had in life.

He stared at his thermos, his eyes glazing over as he realised the awful truth – after today, this was his life. He'd wake up, and she'd *be* there. He'd go to make a sandwich, and the selfish cow would probably insist on making it for him, as if now retired, he was completely redundant.

He'd try to settle down in the living room of an evening to watch his programmes, and then Phil would appear, probably with Barry's favourite, expensive crisps shoved in his mouth, ranting about government conspiracy theories and other such nonsense.

"There you are!" Gladys exclaimed, thudding into the kitchen. "What do you think?"

Barry, with his rucksack in one hand and his thermos in the other, closed his eyes. He often did this when he didn't want her to exist, always hoping that she would somehow melt away before he re-opened them.

"Barry? Are you sleeping on your feet again?"

Barry continued to ignore her for a moment, before realising that there was no escaping her once she'd seen him. He opened his eyes and his mouth dropped open, releasing an unintentional but heavy sigh. Phillip was stood next to her, wearing a suit that was three sizes too big.

"Well?" she pressed. Barry shrugged, with no clue what she was prattling on about. She rolled her eyes and pointed at Phil.

"Why are you awake?" Barry asked, unable to even register that his son was not only conscious, but also dressed. Barry gave him another look, noticing that Phil was wearing one of his old suits. Phil looked as pissed off about wearing it as Barry was to see him in it.

"He's got the job centre this morning," Gladys explained. "He's going on that job seekers."

"Is that right?" Barry replied, following Phil's gaze to the bag of mushrooms on the counter. He stuffed his thermos into his bag and then picked them up, squashing the little things in his hand. Phil grimaced. "You do realise that they'll expect you to actually look for a job?"

With that, Barry headed towards the back door. He didn't dare pass through the kitchen and go out the front way, because that meant heading towards *them* and Gladys would expect a kiss goodbye.

Stuck in traffic, though he'd left a full hour earlier than usual, Barry tapped the wheel and dreaded his day. He was going to arrive late for work, thanks to the ridiculous gridlock that had clearly appeared just to ruin his morning drive. There was no way he'd be able to sneak past anyone either, because it was his last day. Everyone was bound to be hovering around, waiting to congratulate him on his early retirement. He had, of course, been hoping to extend his working life by a few years, if only to stay out of the house a bit longer. But Todd, his new boss Todd, had suggested he 'give himself a break' and finish early.

He groaned as he checked his rearview mirror. A police car was behind him. That wouldn't normally pose a problem, but today of all days he was stuck in traffic with his son's illegal mushrooms sat next to his rucksack on the passenger seat. As far as he remembered, he'd never been in possession of anything illegal in his entire life. He usually just flushed whatever illicit substances he found in Phil's room down the toilet.

It could have been paranoia, but for just a moment, Barry feared that the police officer behind him had felt his nerves. Perhaps he knew, perhaps they had a way of telling when someone had something illegal in their car.

The traffic moved a few inches and then stopped again. Barry glanced down at the mushrooms and into his rearview mirror, getting anxious. The police officer shifted in his seat. Just when Barry was praying for the traffic to move, even at a snail's pace, the driver in front of him switched his engine off. This traffic wasn't going anywhere soon.

Barry could see the headlines now – 'Pensioner Caught with Shrooms', 'OAP Flying High'. Of course he was going to get caught with them, because that was the kind of luck he had. He'd always said that if he didn't have bad luck, he wouldn't have any at all.

As the minutes ticked by, Barry became more and more sure that something bad was going to happen. As if being forced to finish his job and be stuck at home with his wife and kid wasn't bad enough already.

Just as his paranoia pitched, the police officer opened his door and stepped out of his car. And that was it – Barry panicked.

He reached across the seat, his mind a jumble of images of himself in handcuffs and a stripy outfit, and yanked his thermos out of his rucksack and unscrewed the lid. Then, before he knew what the hell he thought he was doing, he tipped the mushrooms out of their plastic bag and into his coffee. Thanks to him pulverizing them in his hand back at home, just to annoy Phil, they fit in nicely.

He screwed the lid on and placed it back on the passenger seat, his heart drumming in his chest like an out-of-time percussionist. He checked his mirror again, breathing a sigh of relief. The police officer was leaning against his car, smoking a cigarette and apparently hadn't noticed Barry's moment of impulsive panic.

Well, his coffee was ruined, and that was something else to add to the list of things that had already been ruined this morning. But at least he wasn't going to prison, Barry figured.

* * *

Almost two hours later, and precisely thirty minutes late, Barry pulled up to the building site, swearing as he noticed that his parking space was taken. He circled around the car park looking for a spot for a while, adding another seven minutes onto how late he was.

Maybe they'll cut me some slack, Barry thought, hurrying to pull himself out of the car. He ran around to the passenger side, flinging open the door and grabbing his rucksack. *Over forty years and I've never been late before, maybe they won't even mention it, and it is my last day after all…*

"Evening, Pufton!" Todd shouted and waved from the site. He pretended to check his watch, which Barry considered stupid, as the boy never even wore a watch. "Nice lie in?"

Todd laughed, along with several others who'd had their attention drawn to Barry's lateness. Barry glared at him, grabbing his thermos, then remembered he couldn't drink his coffee anyway and put it back on the passenger seat. He was about to slam the door, but then something occurred to him. Something devious.

He tried to push the idea away, but his mind was already made up, and with barely a second thought, he picked the thermos back up and slid it into his rucksack. As he hurried across the road towards his co-workers, he caught Todd's eye. For the first time since he'd met him, Barry smiled.

They were building a new housing estate, and the site was busy with the bustle of hard work, the sound of a crane moving girders, and the almost rhythmic music of electric drills.

As it turned out, Barry needn't have worried about being scolded for lateness. After Todd's oh-so-hilarious quip when he arrived, no one had mentioned it. However, as much as Barry hated to admit, even just to himself, he was disappointed that no one had mentioned anything else either. There was no surprise retirement cake, no gift that the boys had chipped in for, no nothing.

By the time lunch rolled around, Barry was in a foul mood. Sat on top of a stack of building materials, he chomped into his sandwich, wondering how the day could be so crap when he was only half way through it. Then he bit his tongue.

Swearing under his breath through a mouthful of bread that now tasted like warm iron, he barely contained his excitement when Todd sat down beside him. Barry watched him as he placed his blue thermos down next to his own, and popped the lid off his plastic tub of chicken salad.

This is it... Barry thought, now smiling through his pain. Suddenly, the taste of blood on his tongue didn't feel so unpleasant. He eyed Todd's thermos, willing him to unscrew the lid, which he did almost immediately.

"You must be feeling great." Todd grinned, turning the lid upside down and pouring himself some coffee. Barry's smile widened. He'd been hoping the kid had brought coffee in all morning. Sometimes Todd had green tea instead, which Barry didn't understand. He'd tried a sip once but it just tasted like dirty water to him.

"The promotion would have felt better, but I suppose," Barry replied, balancing his sandwich on his lap and pouring his own cup of coffee. Todd half-smiled, putting his cup down and reaching inside his jacket. Barry eyed their cups, wondering when the right moment to switch them would come. He didn't have a lot of time.

He might have lost out on the foreman job, and he might have been pushed into early retirement, but thanks to his no-good son he finally had a way to square things up with Todd Tafwell. Now, Barry wasn't familiar with drugs himself, least of all 'magic' mushrooms, but he'd seen Phil reacting to them once.

He'd walked into his son's room, ready to rip his head off for stomping around upstairs like a giant. As it turned out, thanks to adding mushrooms to his pizza, Phil thought he actually was one. Barry had found him holding a mini bottle of whiskey in one hand and a fridge-sized notepad in the other, staring at them in wonder. He'd looked straight into Barry's eyes, happy tears trickling from his own, and asked, 'Dad, have we grown into giants?'

Barry hadn't found that in the least amusing at the time, but the thought of the mightier-than-thou Tafwell boy lumbering around the site thinking he was a fairy or something, and ultimately getting the sack for taking drugs on the job, was almost too good to stand. By the time Tafwell had sobered up enough to try to make sense of it, Barry would be long gone with his retirement package, and who would believe him if he claimed he didn't know how the stuff had got into his system? Phil had taught Barry, if nothing else, that all the kids were into drugs these days.

Todd pulled an envelope out of his inside pocket, and went to pass it to Barry, but a sudden gust of wind took it from his hand. This was the moment – as he leaned to retrieve it, Barry switched the cups.

As Todd returned to his sitting position, envelope in hand, Barry smirked. It was happening. He had to leave today, but the little Tafwell twat would be right behind him. He took another bite of his sandwich, eyeing the cups again, impatient for his revenge to begin.

"This is just a little something for you," Todd said, handing the envelope to him. Barry looked at it with suspicion, taking it out of his hand.

"What is it?" he replied. Todd shrugged.

"A retirement present. Well, a thank you, really. I'll admit I was a bit out of my depth when I got here. Some of the blokes gave me a hard time, but you just got on with it. I learned a lot from you."

Barry opened the envelope, to find the typical 'congratulations on your retirement' card, and a wad of cash inside it that almost matched a month's wage. He looked up at the kid, surprised, unsure of what to say.

Todd smiled.

"Everyone chipped in," Todd added. Barry caught the tremor in Todd's voice, and noticed that the card wasn't signed by anyone else but him. It took just a moment for him to realise that the whole lot was from Todd. He was lying to make him think the rest of them gave a crap he was leaving.

Any reservation that Barry had a moment before about drugging the kid and ruining his career vanished; as well as everything else he hated about him, he now knew him to be a liar too. A *condescending* one, which made it so much worse, Barry thought.

"Well thanks. And I'm gasping here, so cheers!" Barry exclaimed, picking up Todd's cup and raising it high. Todd picked up Barry's cup and raised it. Barry sipped Todd's coffee, hating it because it was smoother and clearly more expensive than the brand he used. Todd brought the cup to his lips, then stopped, sniffing the contents. Barry's heart plummeted as Todd extended his arm and the cup with it, without tasting a drop.

"Sorry, I think we've got mixed up somehow here," Todd explained, handing the cup to Barry and retrieving his own. Barry glared at him as Todd sipped his own coffee. The little bastard. Todd looked up and smiled, though his eyes betrayed his sudden suspicion. "What's in that anyway? It smells weird."

Barry didn't know what to say so he just sat there holding his cup. Todd was right – it did smell weird. That hadn't occurred to Barry, nor had it occurred to him what might happen if Todd realised he was up to something. He thought back to that moment this morning when the sight of the police officer had made him nervous. He was now getting images of new headlines – 'Retired Builder tries to Poison Foreman'.

"I thought you were 'gasping'?" Todd continued. "Come on chap, drink up. Unless…" Todd laughed, "Unless you switched the cups on purpose and there's poison in that one or something!"

Shit. Todd was on to him.

The way Barry saw it, he had two choices; he could refuse to drink his own coffee. With the way Todd was looking at him, he wouldn't be surprised if he confiscated his thermos and had the damn stuff tested. Goodbye prison of his life, hello actual prison. Or, he could drink it and just hope he didn't consume enough for it to have an effect.

The longer he sat there with his cup, the harder Todd stared at him. Barry closed his eyes, hating the guy more than ever before, for putting him in this position. He drank the coffee.

* * *

Barry wasn't sure what to expect. He spent the next twenty minutes paranoid that every gurgle in his tummy meant the mushrooms were kicking in. Then he got paranoid that there was something wrong with his system, because they didn't seem to be kicking in at all. Ten minutes after that, he started to relax. Nothing was happening to him, and he figured that in that small cup there just wasn't enough to do anything after all.

Ten minutes later, as he plodded on with what he admitted was a half-arsed effort in his last few hours of work, he was beginning to forget all about it. That was why he was so surprised when he slid his gloves on and they turned his hands into chocolate.

He stood there, stunned, and stared at his new appendages, wondering how it was possible. He backtracked over what he knew to be true in his mind; when he'd picked the gloves up, they were just bog-standard, thick, brown gloves. But somehow, when they'd slid over his fingertips, they'd melded and become one with his flesh, and then morphed.

Okay, Barry assured himself, *this is fine.* He looked around the construction site, wondering if anyone had noticed what was happening. His concern wasn't that people would judge the change, but that they might be peckish. He laughed.

"Don't be silly!" he chuckled to himself. "Everyone's just had lunch!"

Deciding that his hands were in no danger of being eaten, he decided to just continue with his day, and proceeded to reach for the wooden beam he'd just sanded. He stared down at it, exploding with laughter. He'd had no idea that sanding a simple piece of wood would transform it into a long slab of fudge. Feeling impressed with his workmanship, he looked around.

"Hey! Hey guys!" he called, hoping that someone would come quickly before it morphed back into its original texture. Several of his co-workers looked up from what they were doing, and two of them, James and Paul, wandered over.

"Need a hand?" James guessed, both hands resting on his utility belt.

"I just wanted to show you…" Barry started, then stopped, his mouth falling open as it started to rain. James and Paul looked to the sky, frowning.

"Great, just what we need," Paul muttered, shoving his hard hat onto his head. The rain took Barry aback; he had never seen anything so beautiful in all his life. He looked directly up into it, noting the glistening browns, whites, and blacks as each drop trickled in slow motion from the clouds. As they grew closer, he realised that, like his hands, they were gooey, oozing chocolate pieces.

He lowered his head, ready to rejoice in the change of weather with James and Paul, but Paul's appearance stopped him in his tracks. Suddenly, the world as he knew it started to change.

"You don't look well," Paul commented. But Barry could barely make out the words through Paul's melting lips. As the guy pressed his hard hat onto his head, he started melting into the floor. At first, Barry thought he was merely sinking *through* it, but as he squinted at the vision before him, it became clear that Paul was disintegrating into a bloody mess of liquefied organ and bone.

Barry's eyes widened as the melting mouth continued to ask him what the hell his problem was. Afraid to touch him, lest the peculiar condition was contagious, Barry looked to James for an explanation. Eye contact, he was sure, was key. If he could make eye contact, he could communicate to James that there was something dangerous happening to Paul. Unfortunately though, James no longer had eyes. In fact, he had three mouths, his regular one, and two extra ones where his eyes had once been. It was strange, Barry thought, that he had never noticed that before. All three mouths were licking their lips. Barry wasn't positive, but he suspected that the mouths were intending to devour his hands.

He started to back away, putting his hands behind his back, which was useless anyway since the chocolate had spread upwards, and now his whole arms were chocolate, right up to the shoulders.

"Todd?" all three of James's mouths called. He sounded concerned, but Barry knew better. Todd jogged over, and the sight of him confirmed what Barry had suspected all along. They were against him since the day Todd joined the ranks, all of them. They were all chocolate eaters, they all knew the day would come when they'd be able to gang up and eat him alive, and now it was happening. Barry stared at Todd's head in disbelief that he'd never noticed that he didn't have a face before. He was just a huge, hungry mouth with hair on top.

"It must have been a mask," Barry muttered, still backing away. Before either of them had a chance to try to deceive him any further, he turned and ran in the direction of the first half-built house.

It was difficult to get there, on account of the sticky, thick fudge puddles, but Barry had a strong will to live and for reasons unknown, he was sure that his escape lay in the partly constructed building. A memory was shying just out of reach, a hint to the way out.

He stood in the middle of the house, turning and staring at the two completed walls, and then the empty spaces. He could see more mouths with hair heading in his direction. He'd moved something here earlier, and he needed it. The problem was, he couldn't remember where or what it was.

"Barry!" a voice called, with fake concern. Barry ignored it, shaking melted chocolate rain off his balding head. It was coming back to him now – he was looking for the chocolate portal. It was true that he didn't know what lay on the other side of it, but if he could just make it inside he knew he'd be safe from the chompy teeth that approached.

Finally, he spotted it. It was whirling around in the next building, not this one. *Idiot,* Barry thought to himself. Now Todd and James were directly in his way and he was going to have to get past them. He sucked in a breath and balled his fists at his sides. To his horror, they too started to melt and meld with the rain. Barry shook his head, inaudible words of panic tumbling out of his mouth. He had to get to that portal *now.*

Eyes locked onto the swirling mass of comfort, Barry charged towards it, knocking Paul into Todd and onto his ass as he barged past them.

"Barry, no!" Todd screamed, as Barry reached his destination. In a moment of pure joy, perhaps the only one he had ever felt in his whole life, Barry closed his eyes and dived head first into the portal.

* * *

After the investigation closed, Todd Tafwell decided not to share with the workforce, or anyone else, that Barry had tried to spike his coffee. In respect of the deceased, he reported that Barry Pufton had accidentally ingested a hallucinogenic substance, leading to the situation that caused his death. A lesser man may have divulged Barry's plan, but Todd saw no reason to taint the reputation of the grumpy, old chap, deciding that whatever he'd suffered in those last few minutes was punishment enough. He had an idea of why Barry had attempted to feed him drugs, but what he would never know, for the rest of his life, was why he had dived into that cement mixer.

Kayleigh Marie Edwards

'TWAS THE NIGHT BEFORE CHRISTMAS

'Twas The Night Before Christmas

Dan and Nathan normally loved being in the woods behind their house, but they were hungry, it was getting cold, and daylight was retreating. Plus, their dad, Jim, was getting on their nerves.

It was the day before Christmas Eve, and their mum had sent them out to find a new Christmas tree. They had put their original one up weeks ago, but thanks to the new, grumpy dog that Jim had insisted on adopting, that tree hadn't survived.

Jim had dragged them around every shop he could think of, but this close to the big day, the trees were sold out, and they weren't having much luck. Dan and Nathan didn't care for shops; shopping was never fun for ten-year-old twins. Fearing the wrath of his wife if he returned empty-handed, Jim had decided to drag the boys into the woods to find a real tree instead, and now the boys were trailing behind him looking irritated.

"Dad," Dan whined.

"Dad," Nathan chimed in. "We're bored."

"Yeah," Dan agreed. "Christmas trees don't even grow in these woods!"

Jim looked over his shoulder at his bored sons, their hoods pulled up over their heads. Dan had yanked the drawstrings on his so tight that barely any of his face remained; it looked like his hood was slowly digesting his head.

"Now come on boys! You're supposed to be keeping your eyes peeled!" Jim enthused, holding a leafless branch back for the boys as they stepped into a small clearing. Dan sighed and then Nathan sighed harder. They stared at him.

Jim didn't care for the look they were giving him. It was the look they gave him every time there was going to be trouble getting them to go to bed on time. The look they gave him when they were teaming up to make his life difficult. He wondered if that was even the look they'd given him that time they hid oranges behind the radiator in the living room. It had taken over a month to figure out what the smell was and where it was coming from.

Despite the cold, Jim felt a bead of sweat form above his left eye. He scanned the clearing, relief invading him as he locked eyes on the tree.

"A-ha!" Jim cried, striding over to what appeared to be a Norway spruce, or at least a similar tree that looked just like one. In any case, it looked like a Christmas tree, and it would do.

Dan and Nathan looked around, their joint stare of defiance evaporating in way of nerves. There was something funny about that tree, and they didn't think it was very respectful to hack it down, considering where it was growing.

"Dad, we're not meant to cut trees from this bit of the woods," Nathan informed him. He shifted on his feet, getting a bit closer to Dan so that their arms were touching.

"What are you talking about?" Jim replied, his hands on his hips. He didn't take his eyes off the beautiful eight-footer.

"Dad! We're in the graveyard!" Dan hissed, gesturing towards several hand-made wooden headstones. Jim turned, mildly concerned, noticing the cross-shaped grave markers of all his neighbour's fallen pets.

"Oh yeah, I forgot about this," he muttered. "Isn't this where we buried Bubbles?"

"No, we flushed Bubbles down the toilet so he could go back to the sea," Dan replied, irritated.

"We buried Scratchy here last Christmas," Nathan added, through gritted teeth. Jim saw the flash of anger in his sons' eyes again. He thought the new dog would cheer the boys up after their cat died, but apparently he was wrong. The twins firmly believed that dogs and cats were mortal enemies, and they hated that poor little pug out of some twisted loyalty to their old cat. Jim guessed that was fair because he'd always really hated that cat.

The clawed beast had had it in for him from day one. Every opportunity it got, the damn thing took a chunk out of him. He sometimes wondered if the furry little git knew he hated cats.

"Maybe the tree is a present from Scratchy then? Don't you think that Scratchy would want us to have this lovely tree?" Jim tried. The boys both folded their arms.

"You're not meant to go digging where there are bodies buried," Nathan mumbled. Jim rolled his eyes, wondering where on earth the boys had got that concern. He really had to stop letting them watch horror films.

"Look boys, we can't go home without a tree. And it's the only one we've found, so we're gonna have to take it."

Nathan and Dan looked at the tree for a moment, and then at each other, and then turned their heads back towards Jim.

"But it's weird," Dan said. Jim frowned and shrugged, his 'why?' gesture.

"Because it's the only tree like it growing here?" Dan explained, rolling his eyes. "And, it wasn't even here when we buried Scratchy and it's already grown big. It's weird."

Jim tried to hide his smile, but had to admit to himself that he was a little worried about the boys' paranoid imaginations.

"Okay, we'll leave it then," Jim lied. Satisfied, they all headed back towards their festive, twinkling house. Jim felt guilty about lying to them; it wasn't a lesson he wanted to teach his kids. However, the only way they were going to get into bed without giving him trouble was if they thought he'd agreed with them. Plus, he needed to go back anyway so he could fetch his axe from the shed.

Nathan and Dan woke up at exactly the same time on Christmas Eve. It was still dark out, so they guessed it was around six in the morning. They looked at each other through sleepy eyes from their beds on opposite ends of the room, wondering what had disturbed their slumbers.

They both tilted their heads and frowned, trying to identify what the low, almost rumbling, sound coming from downstairs was. A moment later, they heard a bark. Their eyes met again as they both figured out that the rumbling noise was the dog growling, but that surely wasn't loud enough to wake them up?

The dog barked again, and a new sound drifted up the stairs, a festive sound. Gentle clinking, like when someone taps something on a glass when they're about to make a toast. The sound had a glittering quality to it, the boys thought, if sounds could be described in visuals. They were quite enjoying the peaceful, twinkling sound until it occurred to them that it was the glass tree ornaments rustling and hitting other tree ornaments.

Their frowns deepened. They didn't need to verbalise what they were thinking to each other, because they each knew the other was thinking the same thing. Jim, dear old daddy, had gone back for that creepy tree. Then, he and mum had decorated it with considerable low-noise-level ninja skill while they slept. Well, if either of their parents thought they were going to bed without kicking up some trouble tonight, they could think again. And on Christmas Eve, no less.

Since that stupid pug had taken out the last tree, the combination of sounds was no doubt the horrible little thing having a go at this new one.

The boys climbed out of bed and, in their matching Star Wars pyjamas, tiptoed to the top of the stairs. They peered over the banister into the gloom of downstairs, where they could just about make out a small stretch of the hallway and the open living room door.

There was another bark, and a lot more tree rustling and clinking. Judging by the noise, that dog had probably eaten half the tree by now.

"Sssshhh!" the boys commanded. Just for a moment, there was silence. Then the dog let out a yelp and started growling again. For a small dog, it had a big growl. Nathan and Dan hugged themselves, more out of instinct than cold.

"Let's go down there and shut him in the kitchen," Dan suggested, about to descend the staircase. Before his foot landed on the step, the pug backed out of the living room into the hallway, still growling.

"Stupid dog," Nathan commented. The dog was so focused that it wasn't aware of the boys watching it from their perch on the landing. Nathan and Dan leaned a little further over the banister, wondering why the dog was so annoyed.

It lowered down on its tiny haunches, as if it were gearing up for a fight. The boys waited, expecting to see the dog shoot back into the living room, ready to commence another tree battle. What they didn't expect was to hear the tree rustle even louder than before. Glass ornaments clinked together so loudly that a couple surely smashed, or at least cracked.

The boys looked at each other, hugging themselves tighter.

The dog was now in the hallway.

The tree was still rustling.

Hmmm.

Nathan was about to suggest that perhaps their dad had unknowingly brought some sort of wildlife in with the tree; perhaps a sneaky squirrel? That would explain all the continued movement, and why the dog was so aggravated. It seemed like a totally logical explanation until they realised that not only was the tree rustling and clinking but the sound was actually getting closer.

The dog backed up, almost against the wall.

The rustling grew louder.

The boys looked at each other and then turned to look at their parents' bedroom door. It was closed, and they could hear both their mum and dad snoring inside. Clearly, the boys hadn't inherited their parents' ability to sleep through anything.

The rustling grew louder still.

A glass bauble smashed on the floor.

The dog stopped barking and froze.

The boys looked back down over the banister, frozen, despite the central heating.

Several shapes, like long, pointy, thin arms appeared through the living room door. It was dark down there, but Nathan and Dan knew what they were seeing; it was the tree.

The dog turned tail and fled out of the boys' view into the obscured part of the hallway. The tree followed.

It was slightly too wide for the hallway, and the branches scraped along the wallpaper. Baubles and glass elves and snowflakes clinked together and glittered through the dark as the tree shuffled along in pursuit of the dog.

Nathan and Dan backed away from the top of the stairs, deciding that they didn't want to know. They knew there was something wrong with that tree, but this was too weird, even for them. They usually *liked* weird, but this was just bat shit crazy.

"Are we dreaming?" Dan asked. Nathan shrugged but considered it for a moment.

"I guess so," he replied.

"So what do we do now?" Dan wondered, tapping his finger on his chin, a habit he'd picked up from his dad without even realising it.

"Fight the tree?" Nathan replied, though he didn't sound like he could be bothered to fight anything.

"That's stupid!" Dan laughed. Nathan laughed too, nodding in agreement. The boys ran on their toes back to their beds, tucked themselves back in, and closed their eyes. As they drifted back off to sleep, they both couldn't wait to wake up the next day and tell the other about the bizarre dream.

A couple of hours later, Nathan and Dan woke up in the daylight, excited. They loved Christmas Eve; it was the calm before the best storm ever. The family tradition was to sit in front of the TV all day watching all their favourite Christmas films and eating all of their favourite treats. Christmas Eve and Christmas Day were the two days a year that they were actually allowed to eat chocolate for breakfast.

Mouths watering at the thought of their sugary start to the day, they sprung out of bed and all but sprinted downstairs. But for the first year ever, they weren't met by the jolly, festive, smiling faces of their parents. They didn't reach the bottom of the stairs and charge through the living room into the kitchen, where their breakfast platter of goodies awaited.

They reached the bottom of the stairs to find scratched wallpaper and dirty, dark green smudges all the way down the walls in the hallway. There were pine needles everywhere. Near the front door, there were smashed tree ornaments littering the carpet. The boys noted the immaculate area at the bottom of the stairs, which had clearly been vacuumed to avoid them cutting their feet on the festive debris.

Before they could step foot into the living room, Jim appeared in the doorway.

"Oh, you're awake! I was just coming to get you. Get in the kitchen right this instant, the pair of you!" he barked. Nathan and Dan padded into the living room, their shoulders hunched, and headed towards the kitchen. They both looked into the corner of the room on their way past though. The Christmas tree stood there in its rightful place, exactly where it should be. Considering the mess of pine needles and other bits of tree and shattered ornaments all over the hallway and the living room, the tree itself looked fine, if a little sparse on a few of the branches.

"What the bloody hell did you boys think you were doing last night? What on earth got into you?" their mum demanded. She was leaning against the kitchen counter with her arms folded. She was in her reindeer jumper but her Santa hat was next to the fridge, so she could have only been feeling half-festive, tops, the boys figured.

"I know you didn't want me to get the tree, but you can't just go mental and trash the house because of it!" Jim explained, his voice taking on that 'you're in big trouble' tone and volume.

The boys shrunk against each other.

"We didn't do it," they said. Their parents looked at each other, shaking their heads.

"Oh, and now you're lying too?" Jim fumed. "This is not how you boys were raised. We're going to have to replace the wallpaper in the hallway, and half of the new tree decorations are in bits! And where on earth is the dog?"

Nathan and Dan looked at each other, their jaws dropping open.

"The tree did it," they explained. Their parents exchanged an exasperated, if confused, look. Jim snorted.

"Right, so the tree just hopped out of its pot and took itself for a walk, did it?" he scoffed. Nathan and Dan nodded.

"And we think it ate the dog," Nathan added. It was time for their mum's jaw to drop open. There was a very uncomfortable moment of silence before she let out a huge sigh.

"Right. Both of you get to your room and think about what you've done. You're grounded."

The boys would have argued, but that would have been unwise judging by the glowering expressions on their parents' faces. Plus, they really had no idea how to convince two sane adults that the tree had come to life and battled a pug in the middle of the night. It was utterly ridiculous.

The twins spent a good chunk of the day in their room awaiting some terrible punishment, but eventually, they were allowed to just go downstairs and watch their films and eat their snacks. Their parents, having never had to deal with such naughtiness from them before, didn't really know what to do apart from ground them. Also, after the initial shock and anger had worn off, they really didn't want to ruin Christmas, so they figured they'd deal with it after all the festivities in the New Year.

However, as they sat around the TV, illuminated by the many multi-coloured lights, Nathan and Dan couldn't take their eyes off the tree. They didn't know if the 'incident' of that morning was a one off, or if this tree was mocking them, but it didn't budge an inch all night.

As the night drew to a close, they started to relax, but only a little. They shared a bad feeling.

At around one in the morning, Dan was awoken by rustling, clinking, and shuffling. In his sleepy state, his first assumption was that it was Santa leaving their presents. Excited, he threw his covers off and tiptoed out to the top of the stairs. The memory of the evil, sneaky tree punched him into full consciousness as he reached Nathan, who was wide-awake and already staring down over the banister.

Before they could utter a word to each other, Jim

appeared next to them on the landing.

"What are you two doing out of bed? Santa won't come if you're awake!" he warned. The boys looked at him, their faces as white as the snow that had just begun to fall.

"It's doing it again," Dan whispered. Jim shrugged his questioning shrug.

"The tree," Nathan elaborated. Jim sighed.

"For crying out loud, boys! Not this again!"

"Listen!" Nathan and Dan insisted. They all stood there for a moment, silent. Frustration started to bubble up in the boys, as they heard absolutely nothing.

"Right, let's settle this, come on!" Jim said, plodding down the stairs.

"Dad, no! It will get you!" Nathan hissed, his fingers curling around the banister so tight that his knuckles went white. Jim flicked his hand in the air in a dismissive wave and continued down to the hallway, then left their eyesight as he entered the living room. The light clicked on, but the boys could neither see nor hear anything else happening.

They hesitated for a second and then followed him. They hovered at the living room door for a moment, and then peered inside.

"See, it's just a tree. Honestly, what have you two been watching?" Jim smiled, too tired to be annoyed. "Have you been eating cheese before bed again?"

He walked towards them, intending to scoop them up and carry them back to their beds, when he heard the rustle of branches. The boys' eyes widened as they stared past him towards the tree.

Jim turned, curious as to what had caused the

movement, to find that the tree was no longer standing in its pot, but rather balancing on its severed trunk just in front of it.

"What the...?" Jim trailed off, bending down to inspect how it could possibly be so balanced. The tree should have toppled over without its pot of dirt to root it, but there it was standing perfectly. Jim turned back towards the boys and proceeded towards them. "Okay, I don't know how you did that but..."

Nathan and Dan gasped in unison as the rustling began again. Jim turned quickly, but the tree was static when he slapped his eyes back on it. Only... now it was a couple of inches to his right, and at least a few human steps closer to him. Jim scratched his head and laughed, but it wasn't a laugh of amusement.

"You two have pulled some pranks before but this is..."

"We're not doing it!" Dan hissed, too afraid to be capable of raising his voice above a whisper.

"Yeah Dad, get away from it!" Nathan begged, his eyes like saucers. Jim glanced back at the boys for only a second, but by the time he was facing the tree again it was only two feet away from him.

Jim reached out towards the tree but hesitated before touching a branch. As his fingers grew closer to the pine needles, the branches appeared to bush up, and a peculiar, but recognizable, sound came from the very centre of the tree.

"Dad, don't!" Nathan screamed. But it was too late.

The second Jim's fingers connected with the branch, the tree wiggled, shaking from its core like it was vibrating furiously. And then it lunged.

Jim cried out as the tree took him off balance and landed on top of him. Nathan and Dan stood there watching the impossible, ridiculous attack on their dad. The branches lashed out at him like claws, scratching every bare bit of flesh available. They didn't dare move, but Nathan and Dan had both identified the sound that had come from it right before it lunged – it was a yowl.

They weren't sure how, but the tree was biting him. Nathan nodded to himself, realising that they had been right and this tree had definitely eaten their dog. And now they knew why. Dogs were the mortal enemies of cats.

It was surprising, considering how vicious the attack was, that there was very little blood on the carpet by the time the tree was through with Jim. Besides that bit of red, splattered evidence, there was no trace of him. The boys weren't sure exactly where its mouth was, but the tree sure had a big one.

As the tree wobbled back to a standing position, the boys held their breath, wondering what it would do next. Though the shock of watching a tree devour their dad was sinking in, they were no longer afraid, because now they knew what the tree was.

It seemed to look at them, though it didn't have eyes, and then returned to its pot and replanted itself. The puffed up bushiness of the branches settled, as it seemed to curl up in the pot. Then, as if to confirm their suspicion, it started purring.

Nathan and Dan looked at each other, beaming, then sprinted over to it.

"I knew it!" Nathan cried, stroking one of the branches. The volume of the purring increased.

"Scratchy, it is you!" Dan exclaimed, burying his face in the pine needles. "But how?"

"It's like that film!" Nathan explained, hugging the tree. Dan nodded, remembering their sneaky, late night horror movie viewing from a few months before. Though, in that film, the pets came back in their own bodies. He shrugged, remembering an old guy in the film explaining that sometimes what went in the ground wasn't the same as what came out, and he supposed that that's what had happened here.

Sometimes a tree is better.

ABOUT THE AUTHOR

Kayleigh Marie Edwards is a writer of fiction, reviews, articles, and theatre plays. Finding that horror and comedy tend to go hand-in-hand, she exclusively writes in these genres, and enjoys combining them. She believes that there's no problem in life that can't be solved with a good laugh, or a good scare.

Kill 'em in the Brain – a zombie sitcom - was her first theatre production, and she has since written family-friendly Halloween shows for a holiday park. She has been published in several horror anthologies, and has been placed in several short fiction competitions across the web.

She can be found listing horror movie facts at www.spookyisles.com, and has a page called 'Challenge Kayleigh' at www.gingernutsofhorror.com, in which horror fans challenge her to positively review the very 'worst' movies that the genre has to offer.

She lives alone in her house of horrors with her cat. And she's fine with it.

Original Publications

Original versions of these stories appeared in the following:

Bits And Bobs – Give: An Anthology of Anatomical Entries – When The Dead Books In

Siren – Nightmares and Echoes – GWS Press

Now You See Them – In Creeps The Night – J.A.mes Press

Skin – The Black Room Manuscripts Volume One – Sinister Horror Company

'S' Day – Deluge: Stories of Survivial and Tragedy in the Great Flood – Garden Gnome Press

Barry's Last Day – Death By Chocolate – Knight Watch Press

The Sinister Horror Company is an independent UK publisher of genre fiction. Their mission a simple one – to write, publish and launch innovative and exciting genre fiction by themselves and others.

SIGN UP TO THE SINISTER HORROR COMPANY'S NEWSLETTER!

THE SINISTER TIMES

As well as exclusive news and giveaways in the newsletter we'll also send you an eBOOK "The Offering" featuring nine short stories, absolutely free.

Sign up at **SinisterHorrorCompany.com**

SINISTERHORRORCOMPANY.COM